In the Time of Dinosaurs

rose three metres from the water. A very long
neck. Like a grey-green giraffe. On the end of
that neck was a sculpted, streamlined head
about half a metre long. And coming up, right
behind it, was another tall neck and head.

    <What is that, the Loch Ness monster?!>
Marco cried.

    <They're coming after us!> Cassie said.

knew what it was. Or at least I knew what it
looked like. But I wasn't about to say anything.
If I was wrong, Marco would tease me about it
until the day I died. Besides, it was impossible.
Totally impossible. . .

Look for other ANIMORPHS titles
by K.A. Applegate:

1 The Invasion
2 The Visitor
3 The Encounter
4 The Message
5 The Predator
6 The Capture
7 The Stranger
8 The Alien
9 The Secret
10 The Android
11 The Forgotten
12 The Reaction
13 The Change
14 The Unknown
15 The Escape
16 The Warning
17 The Underground

MEGAMORPHS
1 The Andalite's Gift

ANIMORPHS®

<MEGAMORPHS #2>

In the Time of Dinosaurs

K.A. Applegate

Hippo

For Michael and Jake

Scholastic Children's Books,
Commonwealth House, 1–19 New Oxford Street, London WC1A 1NU, UK
a division of Scholastic Ltd
London ~ New York ~ Toronto ~ Sydney ~ Auckland
Mexico City ~ New Delhi ~ Hong Kong

First published in the USA by Scholastic Inc., 1998
First published in the UK by Scholastic Ltd, 1999

Copyright © Katherine Applegate, 1998
ANIMORPHS is a trademark of Scholastic Inc.

ISBN 0 439 01111 6

Printed by Cox & Wyman Ltd, Reading, Berks.

10 9 8 7 6 5 4 3 2 1

Chapter 1

 Marco

My name is Marco. And I'm the idiot who happened to be watching the news on TV, and happened to see the story about the nuclear submarine that went down.

Do you ever wish you could just learn to keep your mouth shut? I do. At least in this case I did. Because if I'd just kept my mouth shut, I wouldn't have ended up trying to suck air through my blow-hole in the middle of a raging storm that kept dropping ten metre waves on my head.

1

But maybe I should back up. Maybe I should explain why I had a blow-hole in the first place.

I'll make this quick: things are happening here on good old planet Earth. Things most people would never dream of. Things that if you told people they'd say, "Yeah, right. Want to try on this straitjacket?"

We are being invaded. Not by spaceships from outer space firing ray guns. I mean, yes, from spaceships, but mostly the Yeerks don't use a lot of ray guns.

The Yeerks are a parasitic species. Like tapeworms or lice or certain gym coaches who think you can't play basketball just because you are somewhat not tall.

But Yeerks don't crawl on top of your head like lice. They crawl inside your head. A slug like a big snail slithers into your ear, oozes into your brain, flattens itself out, sinks into all the cracks in your brain, and from that point on, controls you. It can even force you to listen to Kenny G.

Actually, it's not funny. I tend to make jokes, especially about things that bother me. And the Yeerks bother me. One of those people who has been enslaved by the Yeerks is my mother. We thought she was dead. She's not. At least I think she's not. When I last saw her she was still alive.

Trying to destroy me and my friends, as a matter of fact.

Which is a lot worse than just being grounded.

Anyway, there are the Yeerks, this parasitic species that rampages throughout the galaxy looking for new host bodies. They control the Gedds, a species from their home planet. They control the Hork-Bajir and the Taxxons. And their target now is Earth and humans.

What does this have to do with me having a blow-hole? Well, there's another species in on this with us. The Andalites. The Andalites are stretched thin trying to resist the Yeerks. An Andalite task force got hammered in orbit above Earth. One of them, Prince Elfangor, made it to Earth and happened to crash near my friends and me. He gave us the Andalite morphing power. The ability to absorb DNA from any animal, and then actually, literally *become* that animal.

We use that power to resist the Yeerks. "We" being Jake, who is our prematurely middle-aged, fearless more-or-less leader; Cassie, our animal expert and tree-hugging environmental wacko; Rachel, Jake's fabulously beautiful but totally insane cousin; Tobias, who's a mouse-eating bird; the Cinnabon-chomping Andalite scorpion-boy we call Ax; and me, Marco, the sensitive, sensible, smart and good-looking one.

Also modest. And honest.

And did I mention cute?

Anyway, I was hanging out with my dad around noon on a rainy Saturday, slumped down in the easy chair, staring at the TV, wondering if I had the energy to go into the kitchen to get more Doritos, when the news flash came on.

A nuclear sub was reported to have developed reactor problems. It was feared sunk. Rescue ships and divers were on the scene, but the storm was making it hard for them. They couldn't find the sub, which could be dousing everyone on board with radiation.

"Oh, man," I groaned.

"Yeah," my dad agreed. He was slumped on the sofa wondering if he had the energy to go to the kitchen and get his Cheez Puffs.

"Um. . ." I said.

"Are you going to the kitchen?" he asked hopefully.

I sighed. "Actually, I just remembered I'm supposed to help Jake with some work over at his house."

"Oh. You'll miss the game," he said. "So before you go, could you grab me the bag of Cheez Puffs? And a drink? And a pillow? And give me the remote control."

I carried about twenty-four items to my dad,

then took off out into the rain to walk to Jake's house. I had to tell him about the sub. I don't know why, I just had to. I guess I thought we could possibly help.

Thirty minutes later, the six of us were assembled on a wet beach. There was absolutely no one in sight. No lifeguards. No little old ladies collecting shells. I mean, it was really raining. We were all soaked through and had wet sand caking our shoes. All except Rachel, who I swear has some magic ability to repel dirt, mud and rainwater.

"Well, we have privacy, that's for sure," Jake said, looking around.

"What are we going to do with our outer clothing and shoes?" Cassie wondered.

See, we can't morph clothing and shoes. Just things that are skin-tight. I was wearing cycling shorts and a way-too-small, totally uncool T-shirt under my clothes. Those I could morph.

"I've said it before, I'll say it again," I said. "We have got to do something about these funky morphing outfits. We are a disgrace to super-heroes. Can you imagine us ever being in a comic book alongside Spider-Man? We'd look like the Clampetts."

"The what?" Cassie asked.

"You know, the Beverly Hillbillies."

"Marco, you do realize that Spider-Man isn't real, right?" Rachel asked. "And even if he was, I don't know what fabric that outfit of his is made from. Never bags at the knees or elbows. I mean, come on."

"We'd better get going before someone shows up," Jake said glumly. Jake hates dark, overcast days. It makes him grumpy.

We stripped off our outer clothes and shoes and stuffed them into a backpack. We stuck the backpack in one of the blue rubbish barrels they had along the beach.

"Maybe we'll get lucky this time and they won't pick up the rubbish today," Cassie said.

"Yeah, it'd be a shame to lose those jeans of yours," Rachel said. "If your legs shrink ten centimetres those jeans would almost fit."

Rachel and Cassie are best friends. But they don't agree on the importance of clothes.

<Come on,> Tobias called down from above. <There are guys out there who might be dying. Let's just get it over with already!>

Floating over our heads was Tobias, a red-tailed hawk. A wet red-tailed hawk. We heard his thought-speak in our heads. We also knew why he was anxious. Tobias does not like the water. But he was trying to act all macho about it.

We waded into the water. Jake, Cassie,

Rachel and me. And Ax. Ax was in his disturbingly attractive human morph. As opposed to his disturbingly disturbing true Andalite body. He had to return to his own form before he could go into another morph. He'd picked up his newest morph at The Gardens — with Cassie's help, of course. Tobias had to morph straight from his hawk shape. Which, as you can guess, is not all that fun, since a hawk in the surf is pretty helpless.

I swam some way with the others. Tobias looked around once more with his hawk eyes and pronounced the beach definitely empty. Then he sighed heavily and plunged into the water.

I focused my mind on the DNA inside me. I formed the picture of the dolphin in my head.

And I began to change.

Now you know how I got a blow-hole.

Chapter 2

 Cassie

I love being a dolphin. How can you *not* love it?

I'm not crazy about morphing insects. Especially the mindless little automatons like termites and ants. But I'm convinced that dolphins have souls. Or maybe it's just some arrangement of DNA-based characteristics that make them seem that way to humans. But whatever it is, whether it's something mystical or something real, I like it.

We were in the surf, breasting the waves and

staggering against the flow. When the cold water was up to my chest I pushed off and swam. It wasn't easy fighting the waves. Humans are not very strong in the water.

As I doggy-paddled, I began to morph. My fingers stretched out longer and longer. A webbing grew between them, like a duck's feet. My arm bones shrank and drew this webbed hand towards my body till it was clearly a fin and not a hand any longer.

My legs softened. Like over-cooked spaghetti, they twined together and melted into the long tail of the dolphin. At the same time my feet twisted outwards and thinned to become the tail flukes.

Then, as I gasped and spat out mouthfuls of salt water, my flat human mouth and face began to bulge outwards. It was like something out of a cartoon. As if I were made of Silly Putty and someone was stretching my face.

My eyes moved to the side and now my vision was largely filled with my own grinning dolphin snout.

More dolphin than human now, I sucked in a last lungful of air through my mouth. When I exhaled, it went out through the blow-hole that had appeared where the back of my neck had been.

9

I dived below the churning surface. I was still in shallow water so I could see the sand and gravel and shells being tugged to and fro by the water.

Humans may prefer shallow water, but it makes dolphins uneasy. So I kicked my powerful tail and headed away from shore.

Think about the happiest day you've ever had in your life. Think of how you feel on a sunny day, with no school and no chores, your pocket money fresh in your pocket and some really fun thing awaiting you. That's exactly what it feels like to be a dolphin.

Then, to all that good feeling, add this sensation of power, ease, of being the perfectly adapted creature in the perfect place.

<Come on, guys!> I yelled, giddy and goofy on the sheer joy of being a dolphin in the sea.

And they came. All of them felt the same way. We were on a serious mission. But that didn't mean we couldn't have fun.

We raced out to sea, surfacing to deliberately plough into the rising walls of waves. We hurried, but we played the whole way.

And then we began to see the helicopters chattering overhead and the Navy ships patrolling back and forth across the sea. The waves were high, the winds, too. When we surfaced it was in the valleys between waves. We'd blow out our stale breath and suck in fresh air, letting the grey waves lift us up so we could see.

<We must be near where they think it is,> Jake said.

<Is anyone else sucking salt water every time they try to breathe?> Marco asked. <Is that good for you?>

<We *are* in the ocean, Marco,> Rachel pointed out. <There's bound to be water in the ocean.>

<Fine, but do we have to be out here in the middle of a storm?>

<Come on,> Jake said. <Let's go below.>

I nosed downwards and kicked. It was much calmer and quieter below the surface. We were in maybe sixty metres of water. It's hard to tell, but it looked that deep, anyway. I was swimming about fifteen metres down and could just barely see the ghostly glimmer of sand far below me. Mostly what I saw was murky blue. Not even many fish.

I fired an echo-location blast from my head. The sound waves spread out, then bounced back. My dolphin brain drew a mental picture of a seabed scarred by a series of deep fissures. I also "saw" divers in the water, and sensors being towed on long cables from the ships above us.

<Even with our echo-location we need to spread out,> Tobias said. <Those fissures are as big as small valleys. The sub could be in one of them.>

<OK,> Jake agreed. <But everyone stay within thought-speak range of the person on your left and right.>

Easier said than done. You ever tried to swim while keeping in line with dolphins on your left and right? Plus we had to surface to breathe, and each time we did the waves would push us forward or back.

Rachel was on my right. Ax on my left. We advanced across the ocean floor, blasting the water with our ultrasonic sound waves.

It had taken forty-five minutes of hard swimming to reach the site. We couldn't go beyond two hours in morph. Not unless we wanted to spend the rest of our lives as dolphins.

Forty-five minutes to get there. Forty-five to get back to shore. That only left thirty minutes to search. Not enough.

But twenty minutes later I saw, or felt, a strange picture in my head. <Hey! Ax, Rachel. I think I've got something.>

I fired a new echo-location blast and "listened" carefully. Yes, something weird. Something definitely weird. Something too "hard".

<Yeah. I have something,> I said. <Rachel, aim a little to your left. Ax, just a hair to your right.>

In a few seconds, Rachel said, <Nothing. I'm not getting anything.>

<I am,> Ax said. <A hard, angular object that appears to be jutting up from the seabed. No, from one of the fissures.>

<I'll take a look,> I said. <It could be just some piece of junk or rubbish.>

I shot to the surface, filled my lungs, and went down. Down and down, till even my dolphin body began to feel the water pressure.

I kept firing echo-locating bursts. And then I was certain. It rose just a few metres from the fissure. But if I recalled my submarine war movies, it was a periscope. The sub's commander must have extended it in the desperate hope that someone would see it.

Someone had. Although not exactly the someone he'd expected.

Chapter 3

Jake

We'd found the sub. Now the question was: how could we get the Navy divers to find it?

<Kidnap one of them,> Rachel suggested.

Rachel almost always likes the direct approach. And in this case, she was right. We needed to get this done and fast. We needed to wrap this up and bail.

<OK,> I said, <we kidnap a diver.>

<What?> Marco said. <You're listening to *Rachel*?>

<She happens to be right,> I said. <Let's go. But don't hurt the person, OK?>

It was easy to find a diver. Their wet-suited bodies and stream of bubbles showed up nice and clear on echo-location.

The diver ignored us as we drew near. We were just a pod of dolphins swimming by. We weren't what she was interested in.

I swam around behind her. The others followed.

<OK, now, we can't help but scare the poor woman, but be as gentle as you can be,> I said. <Grab a leg or an arm. Rachel, help me push.>

One thing you can say about dolphins: there is nothing they can't do in the water. The six of us moved like a well-drilled acrobatic team or something. Hand, leg, hand, leg, we had the diver before she knew what was happening. The others lightly gripped the wetsuit with their dolphin teeth.

"Mblo blo blm blmo!" She yelled. At least that's what it sounded like.

Rachel dug her nose in the small of the woman's back. I nosed her neck, and together the six of us propelled her through the water, almost standing upright, at a speed that must have seemed pretty amazing to her.

She struggled, of course. I think for a

moment she thought we were sharks. I could see wide, scared eyes through her face mask when she turned to look back.

But maybe she'd heard stories about dolphins helping drowning people. Or maybe she just liked dolphins. Maybe it was just so obvious we were on a mission. After a few seconds, she relaxed.

We let her go and I swam up and offered a dorsal fin. She took it. Cassie came up on her other side. And now she co-operated with us, holding on to our dorsal fins as we raced more easily ahead.

We stopped directly over the sub. The diver couldn't see it since it was way below us. But we made a nice show of racing down, then back up, so she'd know what we were doing.

Unfortunately, all this took time. Too much time. We had no choice but to demorph in the open sea.

We swam a kilometre away from the search area and demorphed. Bad for most of us. Worse for Tobias, wallowing with water-logged feathers in salt water. Ax, in his own body, could swim quite well.

We remorphed as soon as we could. And now, with plenty of time, we went back to the site. We had to make sure the divers were there.

<Hey, these guys work fast,> Tobias said when we got back to the site.

A small submersible was already pulling away from the submarine. I guess it was some kind of rescue vehicle for taking people off sunken submarines.

We hovered above the sunken sub. It was wedged deep in the fissure. It was hard to see how they'd ever get it out.

<May I ask a question?> Ax said. <What is the purpose of these submarines? This is a very large craft for simply looking at the seabed?>

A second small submersible was on its way down. It was zipping along. And the divers were all heading for the surface.

I winced. The purpose of this kind of submarine was a little embarrassing to explain to an alien. <Actually, Ax, it's a military submarine. See the rows of hatches along the back? It's a nuclear missile sub. There's a missile under each of those hatches. Armed with a nuclear warhead.>

<Ah. I see.>

<It's deterrence. You know, in case the enemy uses nukes on us, we have these safe on our subs,> Marco explained.

<What enemy?>

<Well . . . OK, we don't exactly have one

right now,> I said, feeling fairly idiotic. <But we used to. And we may get one again.>

<We're shopping all the sales,> Marco said brightly. <Enemies "R" Us, EnemyMart, J.C. Enemy. Don't worry, we'll find one.>

<Are those guys all in a hurry or what?> Rachel asked.

<I was noticing the same thing,> Cassie said. <And look, up above. The ships are all leaving the area. Going in all directions.>

I looked down. The rescue vehicle was already pulling away from the sub. But instead of heading up to the surface, it was simply racing away. Like it was desperate to put some distance between it and the sub.

<I suddenly have a very bad feeling about this,> Tobias said.

<Outta here!> I yelled.

We turned and took off. We powered our tails and tore through the water like torpedoes.

The rescue vehicle was half a kilometre ahead of us. I lost sight of it when we shot to the surface to breathe.

Up, suck in air, down and swim, and up, suck in air, down and swim. It was slower going on the surface, but we needed to breathe because we were straining every muscle in our bodies.

<This is probably stupid,> Rachel said. <I mean, what do we think is going to—>

Flash! A light so bright it seemed to burn right through me.

WHAAAAAAM! The shock wave hit us.

I tumbled through a world that was being torn apart at the seams. And then that world went black.

Chapter 4

 Rachel

I don't know how long I was unconscious. But when I came to I was on the surface of the water. I was lolling there like some kind of dead fish.

First thought: *where are the others?*

Second thought: *how long have I been in morph?*

<Cassie! Tobias! Jake!> I yelled in thought-speak.

No answer. I moved my tail and flippers. OK,

at least I wasn't injured. I dived below the surface and looked around. The water was clearer than it had been. Strange, given the fact that a nuclear warhead had just exploded.

<Marco! Ax!>

<I was wondering when you'd get around to calling *me*,> Marco answered.

He glided up beside me.

<Have you seen any of the others?>

<No. But I was knocked out.>

I fired an echo-location burst. Fish. A pair of distant whales. No dolphins. Although if they were floating on the surface they might not show up.

<I have an idea,> Marco said. <We dive down, then look up. They should be silhouetted against the sun.>

<Good idea. Only it's raining. There's no. . .> I'd been about to say there was no sun. But the golden rays were piercing the water around me. <Must have cleared up. Man, we may have been out a long time.>

We dived down deep. We looked up. And there, outlined against the sun, were four tapered shapes.

<Come on,> I said and shot towards them. I bonked one of them with my nose.

<Hey! What? What?> Tobias yelped. <Jeez!

You scared me to death. Good grief, I thought you were one of those lousy wildcats.>

<Tobias, only *you* would wake up suddenly and worry about wildcats,> Marco said.

<Try sleeping in a tree in the woods,> he grumbled. <You'll worry about them, too.>

We nudged each of the others. Ax and Jake revived. Cassie revived, too. But she woke up screaming in pain.

<Ahhh! Ahhh!>

That's when we noticed the blood leaking from her eyes and blow-hole.

<Oh, oh, it hurts!>

<Demorph!> Jake yelled.

<Trying . . . trying . . . oh, oh!>

Gradually the grey rubbery flesh melted away and a human girl emerged. As she demorphed, the dolphin's pain was left behind. I nuzzled in close, giving her a dorsal fin to hang onto.

"Wow, that really hurt," she said calmly, once her human mouth was back in place. She looked around. "Why is the water so calm? Why is it sunny?" She lifted herself up half a metre out of the water, using Jake and me as support.

Then she settled back. "Um . . . am I awake?"

<Of course.>

"And this isn't a dream?"

<Can't be a dream,> Marco said. <There's

not a single *Baywatch* girl around. Carmen is always there when I dream.>

"You're sure this is reality?" Cassie asked before I could make a crushing remark to Marco about the total impossibility of Carmen Electra ever even looking at him.

<Cassie, it's not a dream,> Jake said.

"OK. Then why is there a volcano over there?"

No one said anything for a few seconds. Then all at once we dived down under, leaving Cassie floundering and yelling, "Hey!"

I dived down seven metres, turned and powered my way straight up. I exploded from the water, smooth and sleek as a missile. I shot up into the air, up where I could see beyond the tops of the short, choppy waves.

I took a look. Then, too stunned to line up for a dive, I belly flopped. The first dolphin in history to belly flop. <There's a volcano over there! There's an actual volcano! We don't have a volcano. I would have noticed that.>

<That was a definite volcano,> Tobias agreed.

<Is it some weird effect from the explosion?> Jake asked. <Like maybe setting off that bomb in the fissure caused some kind of sudden eruption?>

"We have to get back! People could be hurt!"

23

<Something is way wrong here,> I said. <Volcanoes don't just suddenly erupt. Besides, look how high that thing was. That takes hundreds of years of lava and ash building up.>

<How do you know anything about volcanoes?> Jake demanded. <Did we do volcanoes in school?>

<No it was . . . some other place,> I mumbled. But they all just waited. Waited to hear how I knew about volcanoes. <Oh, all right. It was the *Magic School Bus*, OK? They went into a volcano.>

<Excuse me,> Ax said politely. <But something very large is coming towards us. A pair of creatures of some sort. I just echo-located them.>

<A pair of whales,> I said, dismissing it. <I saw them earlier. I think we need to haul back to land and see what—>

<Not whales,> Ax said.

<Who cares? Maybe you missed it, Ax, but we have a volcano — *a volcano!* — right about where all our houses should be! Let's get going. Cassie, you need to—>

"Uh . . . what is that?" Cassie asked. She was staring hard, but she started to morph back into dolphin.

<What?>

"*That!*"

I turned to follow the direction of her stare. We all turned.

It rose three metres from the water. A very long neck. Like a grey-green giraffe. On the end of that neck was a sculpted, streamlined head about half a metre long. And coming up, right behind it, was another tall neck and head.

<No way,> Tobias whispered.

<What is that, the Loch Ness monster?!> Marco cried.

<It's Visser Three in morph!> I said. <No, wait, can't be. There are two of them.>

<No *way*!> Tobias said again.

<They're coming after us!> Cassie said.

<As I said,> Ax said smugly, <*not* whales.>

Chapter 5

 Tobias

I knew what it was. Or at least I knew what it looked like. But I wasn't about to say anything. If I was wrong, Marco would tease me about it until the day I died. Besides, it was impossible. Totally impossible.

So I didn't say anything.

But oh, man, I hauled my dolphin tail out of there.

<They're too fast,> Jake said. <Man, they're fast!>

26

We were ploughing up the now-placid water. We were going flat out. But the creatures were gaining on us. And the whole time in my head I was going, *No way, no way.*

And yet with each glance at those long necks, with each flash of those snake heads, I became more convinced.

The creatures were no more than thirty metres back.

<We can't out-run them,> Jake said grimly. <We either have to split up or fight.>

<Fight!> Rachel said. <They're just some kind of big squid or something probably. Let's get them!>

I liked Rachel even before I became a hawk. But now I really like her. She could be a bird of prey. She'd be a natural.

But she was wrong this time.

<Split up,> I said. <I don't think we can beat them.>

<We haven't tried yet,> she said.

<You don't understand. Look, I know this will sound crazy, but—>

SHWOOOOSH!

Coming up from below. Like some weird, massively oversized dolphin. Fifteen . . . twenty metres long! An impossibly huge jaw open wide.

We'd been watching the creatures chasing

us. All I had time to see of this new threat was the flash of teeth.

<Aaaahhhh!> It had me. No time to move. Up, up, up I went! High into the air, trapped in those massive jaws as it broke the surface.

It tossed me up. Just like I'd seen seabirds do with a fish. Tossed me up, opened its massive jaws, and swallowed me whole.

I was being swallowed!

I was unconscious, then conscious again, then unconscious.

I hit water. No, not water! Too warm. Hot. Burning! My skin was burning!

I was blind. Deaf, except for the sound of churning. And the steady bass drum of a heart beating.

Then, something else beside me. My dolphin sense knew. It was another dolphin. <Who is that?>

<It's me!> an enraged voice cried.

<Rachel!>

<Who did you expect? Jonah? We have to get out of this thing. Ahhhh! My skin is itching and burning.>

<Stomach acid,> I said. <It's digesting us.>

<It's not digesting *me*!> Rachel said. <I'm gonna morph! I'm tearing a hole out of here.>

<You have to pass through human to morph,>

I said. <The stomach acid!>

<No choice.>

I could already feel her changing. I felt human fingers pressed against me in the gnashing, enclosed space. She was right. No other choice. And I wasn't going to let her do it alone.

I had very few morphs available to me. And only one that would help here. But first I had to revert to bird form.

Something like a rock was in the stomach. It was grinding against me with the movements of the stomach wall. And as I lost the tough hide of a dolphin and regained the fragile hollow bones of my own hawk body, the beating became deadly.

Even Rachel's body was crushing me, as her elbows and fists and knees were shoved against me, time and again.

But all that was nothing compared to one simple fact: I couldn't breathe.

Suffocating!

<Air!> I moaned.

Rachel couldn't answer. She was human again. But I knew she must be suffocating, too.

My left wing was broken. My tail was a mess. I was wracked with pain. But none of that mattered because I was going down now. Sinking and swirling down a long, black well.

Too late to morph again. I knew it. I was done.

And my last conscious thought was a flash of myself, years earlier, back when I was still completely human. I saw myself playing with the little plastic figurine — a plastic toy model of the animal whose belly I was in. A booklet had come with the figurine. I'd memorized all the facts in that booklet.

<They were wrong,> I thought as my mind shut down. <It's bigger than they said.>

Chapter 6

 Jake

<It has Rachel and Tobias!> Cassie screamed.

I knew. I'd been on the surface when the monster had snatched them up and tossed them down its throat. But I couldn't think about that. I still had three people with me. I had to save them.

The long-necked creatures were behind us, the larger one in front. Which would eat us?

<Everyone dive!> I said.

<What about—?> Marco began.

<Do it!> I roared.

Down we went. Down fifteen, twenty, twenty-five metres. The monsters were like ships overhead. The two long-necked ones started to dive after us. Then they hesitated. The larger creature, the one that had got Rachel and Tobias, was closing in.

<Now! While they're arguing over who gets to eat us,> I said. <Let's get out of here!>

<We can't leave Rachel and Tobias,> Cassie said.

<Can you beat that thing, Cassie?> I demanded. <You want to stay here and try? Sooner or later those creatures will decide who we belong to. We have to run while they're fighting over us.>

<Rachel!> Cassie cried in thought-speak. <Rachel! Can you hear me? Rachel!>

<Now, Cassie! Marco, Ax, get her!>

Marco and Ax each bit down on a flipper and dragged Cassie away.

<Let me go! Rachel! Rachel! RACHEL!>

I felt sick inside. Mad at Cassie, scared, beaten, and for some reason even mad at Rachel and Tobias. But mostly I felt sick. What was happening?

We swam away as fast as we could move. I heard a screeching roar of rage reverberating through the water. The monsters were fighting.

We swam towards shore. And after a while Cassie swam on her own.

The sea floor beneath us sloped up and up, rising to meet us. When we were in no more than two metres of water, we began to demorph. I hoped we could do it. I didn't know how long we'd been in morph.

I gratefully resumed my own body. I lifted myself sluggishly out of the water and staggered up the beach. I flopped face-down, then rolled over.

Cassie and Marco came seconds later. Ax took a few extra minutes and appeared in human morph.

"Something is very wrong, Prince Jake," he said.

I didn't answer. Of course something was wrong. Rachel and Tobias were probably dead. So something would always be wrong now. For ever.

"Jake, Ax is right," Marco said. "Get up. Look at this!"

I stood up. Marco, Ax and Cassie were all staring, open-mouthed, across the beach towards the boardwalk.

There was no boardwalk.

No hot dog stands, no Ferris wheel, no video

arcades. No buildings at all. No people. Nothing but a line of trees pressing right up against the sand. And off above the trees, the cone of the volcano with a tall plume of smoke.

"This isn't home," Marco said.

"What is going on here?" I wondered. I slogged up the beach towards the trees. I expected to see something behind the trees. But behind the front row of trees were just more trees. Far off, through gaps in the tree trunks, I caught glimpses of an open space. But I was seeing grass and flowers there, not a city.

Marco and Cassie came up behind me.

"Listen," Marco said.

"Listen to what?"

"The quiet. Just the breeze in the trees."

Cassie said, "No seagulls. There are always gulls."

I had noticed something else. "There's no rubbish. No old drinks cans. No sweet wrappers. Nothing. I mean, *nothing*."

"So, what happened?" Marco asked. "That explosion blew us halfway around the planet to some desert island somewhere in the middle of nowhere?"

I shrugged. Most of my brain was still focused on Rachel and Tobias. I wasn't tracking. And yet I felt a nagging sense of urgency. A little voice telling me to get it together. A little warning voice telling me we were not safe.

I turned round. "Ax! What are you doing?"

He was about a hundred metres down the beach. "I'm trying to understand something, Prince Jake."

I headed towards him. The sand was darker and rougher than I remembered. But then, who knew where we were? The tracks I saw in the sand seemed to have been made by large birds. I got this sudden, illogical rush, thinking maybe they'd been left by Tobias. They looked like they'd been made by talons.

But of course that was impossible. I had got Tobias and Rachel killed. If only I'd been watching ahead instead of looking behind, I could have seen the threat coming. I should have had everyone morph to shark. Then we could have fought.

Should have, should have.

"No footprints," Cassie said. "No human footprints, anyway."

We reached Ax. He was staring towards the trees. I followed the direction of his look. There was a sort of alleyway through the trees. Some were bent aside. Some had the branches on one side broken, hanging limp with dying leaves. Other trees were simply snapped. Broken.

And all along this "alleyway" the top third of the trees seemed to have been stripped of leaves.

Marco stared, too. He bumped into me and shoved me into a hole in the sand. I was going to shove him back, but this was no time to be playing around.

"I am still unfamiliar with some Earth creatures," Ax said. "Cuh-ree-chers. Tell me, what sort of creature can do that?"

"Probably a tornado or something," I said vaguely. "I've seen things like that on TV when there's been a tornado."

"Ah," Ax said. "Does a tornado have feet?"

I almost smiled. "No. A tornado is a wind storm."

"I see. Then this was not caused by a tornado. Whatever did this has feet."

"How do you know?" Cassie asked.

"Because Prince Jake is standing in one of the footprints."

I looked down. It could have been the footprint of an elephant. Except that the toes were more like claws.

Plus, the print sank at least fifteen centimetres into the sand.

And oh, yes: it was about a metre and a half across.

Chapter 7

 Cassie

Jake jumped up out of that footprint like it was filled with rattlesnakes.

We stared at the footprint.

Then we looked up and stared at the alley-way that something had made through the trees.

Then we stared at the way the leaves had been stripped from a lot of the highest branches of the trees.

"Jake, something ate those leaves," I pointed out.

"Those trees are like ten metres tall," Jake said.

"There are a cluster of these same footprints over there." Ax pointed about three metres away. "And all across there it's as if the sand has been swept. Swe-put. Swep-tuh."

Jake looked at me. "Cassie, do you know anything that could possibly have this footprint?"

Jake thinks I'm some kind of animal expert. I shook my head. "What it looks like is some very, very large animal came through those woods. It was munching the top leaves of the trees. Like a giraffe would do. Then it hit the water here. It turned round. That's the cluster of prints there. And it has an insanely long tail. That's the swept area. Once it was turned round, it went back the way it came."

"A giraffe?" Jake asked.

"Not a giraffe," I said.

Jake looked a little confused. We all were, but he's the one who gets stuck making the decisions. I felt sorry for him. He'd been right to drag me away from those sea monsters. I should have told him that.

But poor Rachel. Poor Tobias. What was I ever going to do without Rachel? Rachel had been my best friend for ever. I couldn't imagine not seeing her every day.

I realized I was crying. I guess I had been, off and on, since we'd dragged up out of the sea.

I felt Jake's arm go round my shoulders. "Don't cry, Cassie. Don't give up on Rachel and Tobias. You know Rachel. If there's a way to survive, she'll find it."

I wiped my tears. "Yeah. You're right. And we have to focus here."

He took his arm away and suddenly seemed awkward. I think he expected Marco to make some smirky remark. But Marco has a good heart. He knows when to let things go. Besides, I knew Marco was almost as sad as I was.

"What should we do, Prince Jake?" Ax wondered.

"Have I mentioned don't call me prince?" Jake said automatically.

"Yes, Prince Jake, you have."

Jake looked around. "I guess we go that way," he said, pointing to the forest. "But not along *that* path. Whatever crushed those trees and made these tracks, we don't want to run into it. But obviously, wherever we are — some island somewhere, Africa, South America — wherever we are, there have to be people, right? Just not here on the beach. So let's go find them."

I found myself looking back at the sea, at the surf that lapped almost peacefully on the coarse dark sand. Was she still alive somehow? Jake was right: if anyone could get swallowed by a whale — or whatever that thing had been — and survive, it was Rachel.

"I caught a glimpse of a clearing way back in the trees," I said. "Could be a village there."

Jake led the way into the trees. The sun was shut out by the tall, spreading branches. There were vines hanging down and crawling up the trunks of trees. And huge ferns so big you could hide in them.

We struck a stream, maybe five metres across. Both banks of the river were lined by magnolias, dogwoods, and massive fig trees.

"This is not anywhere near being home," I said. "This is more like tropical vegetation."

"It's humid enough, that's for sure," Marco complained.

"I wonder if the water's OK to drink?" Jake asked. Then, with a shrug, he dropped to his knees and dipped his hand in. He brought the water to his mouth and sipped.

"I guess we can always get a bunch of shots for whatever disease is in the water," I said. I dropped beside him and tasted the water. The humidity hadn't seemed so bad down by the ocean. But now it was dehydrating me. I was massively thirsty.

"It's probably OK," I said. "Usually running water—"

FWOOOSH!

A huge head exploded from the water.

SNAP!

A jaw two metres long slammed shut with a sound like steel on steel. The jaw snapped shut so close to my face that it grazed my nose.

I leaped back. Fell on my butt. Spun, jumped up and bolted.

"That was one big honkin' crocodile!" Marco yelled as he ran beside me.

We stopped beneath a huge tree. Four of us, all panting.

"That wasn't right," I gasped.

"Yeah, no kidding," Marco said.

"No, I mean it was too big. The jaw was too long and thin."

"I am really not liking this," Jake muttered. "What were those things in the ocean? What made that footprint? Where on Earth are we that has crocodiles that size? I mean, we've seen crocodiles. That was one way, *way* big croc."

"Prince Jake, I am going to demorph," Ax said.

"Have you been in morph too long?" Jake asked with a frown.

41

"No. But I am frightened," Ax replied. "I don't want to have to fight in this weak human body."

"Yeah, go ahead," Jake said. "Cassie, I don't mean to hit you with this, but you know more about animals than any of us. Where the — where on Earth are we?"

"I don't know," I admitted. "Giant crocodiles, huge, aggressive whales or what ever, like nothing I've ever even heard of, and something big enough to leave a footprint you could turn into a paddling pool. I just don't know."

"OK, fine," he said, obviously frustrated. "Let's try it another way. Ax, you know more about physics and so on than any of us—"

"More than *any* human," Ax said. He was demorphing but was still mostly human.

"What ever. Just tell me how an explosion could have blown us all the way to, I don't know, Madagascar or wherever, without killing us."

"Madagascar?" Marco asked.

"It couldn't," Ax said simply.

"Great. Great. That clears everything up just fine. This is nuts." He sighed. He looked at me and shrugged.

"I don't know," I said. "Maybe when we find some people they can tell us where we are."

We walked on, heading towards the clearing. The forest had become a frightening place to us.

Everything was wrong. Out of place somehow, in some way I couldn't quite explain. How had the storm and rain suddenly become humid sunlight? How had we gone into the water off a beach fronted by a boardwalk and come out at a beach fronted by forest?

"Maybe it's all a dream," Marco said, as if he'd been reading my thoughts. "In which case, I'd like to dream about a nice, ice-cold Coke." He held out his hand, curved around an imaginary bottle. "Hmm. So much for the dream theory."

We were almost to the clearing now. I could see bright, buttery sunlight through the trees. But massive ferns blocked my view of the clearing itself.

"Let's get out from under these trees," I said. "We'll think better in the open. And maybe there will be some people."

"Too bad they'll speak Madagascarese," Marco said.

"Shhh!" I froze.

"What?"

"Shhhh! Listen!" A grunting, snuffling sound to our left. Then the sound of greenery being rustled. Then more snuffling. The sound of . . . eating? "Something munching leaves," I said.

"There's been way too much munching already," Marco muttered.

"No, it's OK," I said. "If it eats plants, it won't eat *us*. Could be a cow. If it's a cow, maybe it belongs to someone."

"And if it doesn't belong to anyone, maybe we can eat *it*. I'm starving."

We threaded our way cautiously towards the sound. The closer we got, the more confident I was. Yes, something was grazing. But did cows eat leaves? No. Deer, maybe?

I pushed aside a fern frond. And there it was.

It was perhaps seven metres long from head to tail. It stood on four elephant-like legs. It had a long neck that made up a third of its length and was balanced by the long tail of equal length. Along its back were bumpy, bony things, like armour plating that only covered that one area.

For about two minutes I don't think one of us drew a breath. We just stared.

"I think it's a baby," I said.

"A baby?" Marco said. "Cassie, it's a dinosaur."

Suddenly.

Crash! Crash! CRASH! CRASH!

From behind us!

"HuuuuRROOOOAAARR!"

The ground shook from the impact of its huge, taloned feet. The blast of its roar shivered the leaves and buckled my knees.

I spun around just in time to see it leap.

It jumped over us like we weren't even there. Jumped over us with its awful, hawk-like talons. It landed with one huge foot on the ground and one holding the side of the "little" dinosaur.

Down came the head. That huge square, familiar head.

The Tyrannosaurus opened its massive jaws and closed them at the base of the baby dinosaur's neck.

I didn't know what was happening. My mind was gone. Gone in out-of-control terror.

We ran.

Chapter 8

 Rachel

I was human! A human gasping for air inside the belly of the creature.

My lungs were screaming and heaving. I was blind. My skin was burning. I was being pummelled, crushed, smashed, beaten.

I was getting mad.

I knew Tobias was there, too, but I had no idea where. He wasn't thought-speaking.

Morph! I told myself. But already I was weakening. The human body can't last long without air.

I tried to focus. But my head was swirling. I wanted to just give up. Why fight it? I was done for.

Not yet, you're not done for, Rachel, I told myself. *Not yet. I might not survive, but by God, I was going to deal with this creature before I went down.*

From far off I could sense the changes occurring. I knew I was growing. But too weak . . . too weak . . . no time . . . no time. And once I dug out I'd find water. Not air.

Air. I needed air. Some nagging part of my brain kept saying, "Lungs!"

I felt like saying, "Yes, I know. I'm suffocating. I know all about my lungs. They hurt. They're heaving, gasping, crying for air."

And I swear, as I swirled down into the darkness, there came a voice, clear as a bell in my head. My own voice, but from outside of my own head.

"No, you idiot," it said. "Not *your* lungs. Duh."

It was the weirdest thing. But suddenly I could see myself clearly. I even knew that I was half-way morphed. I had blonde hair on my head and coarse brown fur on my face. I was crushed inside the gizzard of the beast. A tiny, crumpled bundle of feathers was pressed against me.

I could see it all. But better than that, I could see what the voice meant. I was enclosed in a cage made up of massive ribs. But right there, just thirty centimetres away, was air.

I drew back my massive paw. The paw of a grizzly bear. A paw that could destroy a man with a single, back-handed swipe. I drew that paw back and I extended my wicked, hooked claws, and I thrust that paw straight out. I twisted and pushed. The twist ripped and the power of the thrust dug my paw deep into the creature's insides.

"HREEEEE-UH!"

I heard its scream. It reverberated through the flesh that pressed all around me.

I thrust and twisted.

"HREEEEE-UH!"

Another scream. A spasm that wracked the body so powerfully it almost knocked me out.

But I was not so easily crushed now. I was no longer human. I had finished morphing the grizzly bear. And not even this sea monster could digest a grizzly bear.

With my last gramme of strength, I thrust and twisted.

SHWOOOOOSH!

Air!

Air poured in. I gasped at it. Air!

I had done it. I had ripped a hole out of the gizzard and penetrated the creature's lungs.

<Tobias! Breathe! There's air!>

I went back to work, ripping now with both huge paws. Digging downward to avoid the ribs.

Suddenly water gushed in. Salt water. Cold and wonderful. I kicked and clawed the opening until it was bigger. Then I tumbled out. I hit bottom. I looked up, dazed and disorientated.

The creature had beached itself. I was in no more than two metres of water. I stood up, my huge bear head broke the surface, and I reared up on my hind legs.

Tobias was fluttering weakly in the water. I grabbed him up as gently as I could with bear paws. I lumbered towards shore and set him down on dry land.

<Tobias, are you OK?>

<Do I look OK?> he asked.

<Well. . .>

<Busted wing. Feathers a mess. Half my tail feathers ripped out or eaten away by stomach acid. I'm a definite mess. On the other hand, I'm alive.>

<Yeah,> I said. I reared up to my full height and took a look around. I could tell that we had run up into the mouth of a river.

The riverbanks were steep on our side of the

river. My pathetically dim bear vision could barely make out some vague shapes moving on the far bank. I sniffed the air. The grizzly sense of smell is excellent. What I smelled was puzzling. <I'm smelling . . . I don't know what. It's like something is missing. Like the air has been scrubbed clean. I smell various trees and plants, but. . .> I shook my huge head. <I don't know. Something I should be smelling, only I'm not.>

Tobias stood up shakily on his talons. <Car exhaust? The smell of fossil fuels burning? The faint smells of swimming pools and grease-belching fast-food restaurants? The smell of human sweat, perfume, rubbish? In other words, all the smells of civilization?>

<Yeah. Exactly. You're right.> I glared at him. <Too right. How did you know? What's going on, Tobias?>

<Well, my wings and tail are a mess, but my eyes are still working. I can see what you can't.>

<You can't *see* smells.>

<No. But I can see that small herd over across the river. That small herd of hadrosaurs over there.>

<What is a hadrosaur?> I demanded. I was getting annoyed at the way Tobias sounded. Like he was about to say something important, only he couldn't quite spit it out.

<Hadrosaurs were a group of duck-billed dinosaurs.>

<Tobias, would you mind making just a little bit of sense? Dinosaurs?>

<Yeah. And let's see, if I remember my old dinosaur books, those long-necked things in the water were Elasmosauruses and the thing that you just chewed a hole through was probably a Kronosaurus.>

<Yeah. Right.> I waited for him to laugh at his own joke. Only he didn't laugh. <Dinosaurs?>

<Yeah. Dinosaurs.>

<Oh, man. Tobias, we are gonna need some better morphs.>

Chapter 9

 Tobias

I was in pain. I didn't want to mention it, though. What was the point?

I had very few morphs, unlike the others. We were on land now. A dolphin morph wasn't any use. The only useful morph I had was my human one.

But somehow a human body seemed pathetically weak in a world of dinosaurs. At least in my own hawk body I could fly away from danger.

Unfortunately, my hawk body was a mess.

<Now what do we do?> Rachel wondered. <What about the others? Do you think they made it?>

<I don't know.> I tried to extend my broken wing. <Ahh!>

<Does it hurt?>

<Not really,> I lied.

High above me the huge bear head looked down at me. <Why don't you morph to human, then morph back to your bird body? The new hawk body will be constructed from the DNA and should be fine. Just like what happens when we injure a morphed body.>

<OK.>

It felt weird going human. I'd only done it a few times since the Ellimist had given me back my morphing power.

Now I felt my feathers itching as they melted into flesh. My sight grew dim, my hearing became muddy. I rose up, tall, large, clunky, awkward . . . human.

"At least the pain is gone now," I said. "Now to get feathery again."

A few minutes later, I was my normal — OK, my abnormal — self. Unfortunately. . .

<Aaaaahh! Oww! It just hurts worse!>

<This makes no sense!> Rachel said, sounding outraged.

I laughed grimly. <Rachel, in case you haven't noticed, our lives stopped making sense that day we walked through the construction site and had a spaceship land in front of us. Maybe it's some effect from the time travel — if that's what's happened to us. I'll be sure and ask Ax, if we ever see him again. Or maybe the Ellimist messed me up when he gave me back my powers. It'd be a relief to think that guy is capable of screwing up.>

<Then morph to human. We have to get going. Don't ask me where.>

<No. I need to heal. That will take time. I have to stay in my own body for it to heal. But first I need you to set my broken wing.>

<What? I'm not Cassie!>

<You've seen her do it. So have I.>

<Oh, man,> Rachel moaned. <What am I going to use for bandages?>

<Part of your morphing outfit. That and some twigs.>

<Oh, man,> Rachel said again. <I wish Cassie were here.>

She began to demorph. The massive shoulders and head, the lumbering haunches, the shaggy fur, the huge, powerful paws, all shrank and melted. Gradually a very beautiful human girl emerged.

Rachel looked down at her morphing outfit.

It was a black, one-piece leotard. "OK, so I go to the bare midriff look," she said.

She tried to tear a hole in the fabric. "My fingernails are too short."

<Here. Bend down.> She bent close and I used my beak to make a tear in the fabric.

From that first tear Rachel quickly ripped off three strips of black nylon. "I just have one thing to say, Tobias. Don't break another wing. I mean, this doesn't look bad — it could actually be kind of a fashion statement — but any more and we'd be getting embarrassing."

<Hey, I'm a hawk, remember? I would never even look.>

"Yeah, right." She gathered up some twigs that had been deposited along the river's edge. "What do you think? These OK?"

<Should be. Now, look, all you have to do is straighten out my wing. Make sure the bone is lined up straight. Otherwise it'll heal crooked and I'll spend the rest of my life flying around in circles.>

Rachel looked alarmed.

<Just a joke, Rachel,> I said. But silently I added, I *hope*.

She took my broken wing very gently. "I can tell where it's broken. I'll straighten it, then put a stick on each side and tie it up, right?"

<Yep. Nothing to it.>

Rachel took a deep breath. "On the count of three. One . . . two. . ."

<Aaaahhh!> I yelled, as sharp pain shot up my wing.

"Sorry! Sorry!" she cried.

<Just get it over with!> I yelled.

She held the bone in place with one hand. It hadn't broken into separate pieces, it had just snapped. But it was agonizing. No matter how she tried, she couldn't keep from bending the bone slightly.

She grabbed the two sticks with her left hand and managed to line them up against the bone. She transferred the pressure to her left hand and there came a new wave of pain, so severe it made me sick inside.

She quickly wound one strip around my wing.

<Tighter,> I said.

"It'll hurt you."

<It'll hurt worse if my wing doesn't heal.>

She tightened and I tried not to scream.

The other two strips went on more easily. She checked the knots, then sat back and wiped her face with the back of her hand. She was sweating and pale.

"I don't know how Cassie does things like that," she said.

<You did great. No training, no experience. Come on, you did great.>

She stood up, and for the first time with decent eyes, looked across the river at the small hadrosaur herd. "Oh, my God. What is this, *Jurassic Park*?"

<Probably more like Cretaceous Park. I think hadrosaurs were more common in the Cretaceous Period.>

Rachel glared at me. "I've known you a long time, Tobias. I don't remember you ever talking about dinosaurs."

<I was so into dinosaurs when I was little,> I said. <I was staying with my uncle at that point. He liked to drink. He'd sit in his recliner and start yelling at the TV and cursing, and then yelling at me if I made any noise. I used to go into my room and sit there, playing dinosaur.>

We started to climb up the bank of the river. Or to be more accurate, Rachel started to climb, and I perched like so much dead, useless weight on her shoulder.

It was a struggle to hold on without digging my talons into her skin. I'm sure I hurt her. But Rachel, being Rachel, said nothing.

We reached the top of the bank. We were in a sea of grass that extended alongside the riverbank. Beyond the grass was a line of dark, forbidding trees. Here and there I saw flashes of colour: flowers. And then there was the volcano.

<Flowers,> I said. <Cretaceous Period.>

"So what's the difference between Jurassic and Cretaceous?"

<Well, a lot of things. Cretaceous was the last age of dinosaurs. They died out very suddenly at the end of the age, about sixty-five million years ago. I mean, well . . . sixty-five million years before our own time.>

"So in the Cretaceous Age there's probably just the left-over dinosaurs. Not like the ones in *Jurassic Park*."

<Not exactly,> I said. <See, *Jurassic Park* was slightly inaccurate. I mean, some of the dinosaurs they showed were actually from *this* time, from the Cretaceous.>

She looked hard at me. "You're not going to tell me what I hope you're not going to tell me, are you?"

<Afraid so. If I'm right and we are in the Cretaceous Period, well then, this is the age of the most relentless, powerful, dangerous, ruthless predator in all of history. This is the age of Tyrannosaurus rex.>

Chapter 10

 Marco

CRASH! CRASH! CRASH!

The ground shook!

"HrrrrRRROOOOAAAARRR-unh!"

It was so loud it had to be right behind me!
I was screaming. I was crying as I ran. It was
panic. Pure panic. Leaves slapped my face.
Twigs whipped my bare arms.

I glanced back. Through my blurring tears I
saw it bounding, leaping, running after us.

Thirteen metres long, from head to tail. Six

thousand kilogrammes. Fifteen-centimetre, serrated-edged teeth.

But it was the eyes that were the worst. They were intelligent, eager eyes. Hungry eyes. Eyes that seemed almost to laugh at me, helpless creature that I was.

Could I morph? Morph what? Morph *what*? There was nothing that could stand against a Tyrannosaurus rex. Nothing! My gorilla morph? The Tyrannosaurus would eat it in two bites.

I saw flashes of the others, all in flat-out panic run. It would have us all. None of us could fight it. Not even Ax, who was pulling ahead of the stumbling humans.

No! Wait! There was a way!

"Get small!" I screamed. "Morph small!" The words tore my throat as I yelled.

Wham!

The root seemed to reach up out of the ground to grab my foot. I hit hard. I sucked air but nothing came. My lungs were emptied. Heart pounding. The others kept running. Didn't realize I'd fallen. Roll!

I rolled over just as the impossibly big talon came raking down.

WHAMMM! The tyrannosaur's foot hit like a dropped safe. I bounced from the impact.

Down came the head, teeth flashing, eyes greedy for my flesh.

I sucked in a breath. Rolled, scrambled, tripped, kicked forward and landed in a fern at the base of a tree. The tree trunk was no more than a half-a-metre in diameter.

I pulled myself behind it. No way to hide.

The dinosaur kicked at me with one foot. I dodged.

"Morph, you idiot!" someone yelled at me. I recognized my own voice, but I couldn't imagine speaking the words.

What? What could I morph? What was small enough?

SCRRRRRAACK! WHAAAMMM! A talon came down and scraped the bark off the tree before it hit. I yanked my leg out a split second before it would have been crushed.

Talon? Yes, huge bird feet. Bird, that was the trick. See if the big, evil creep could fly!

I focused some part of my mind on the image of an osprey. Small, too small for the T-rex to care about. And it could fly.

I felt the changes begin, but the Tyrannosaurus hadn't got to be the biggest flesh-eater in history by being stupid. It came round the tree for me. And now my body was growing clumsy as my hands shrank and my legs thinned.

You have no concept of how powerful that Tyrannosaurus was. You cannot possibly even begin to understand till you've cowered beneath it, peeing in your pants, and wanting to dig a hole in the dirt.

I scrambled round the tree. Jaws opened a metre and a half wide and snapped shut half a centimetre from my head.

"Aaaahhhh!" I screamed in sheer terror.

The big lizard dodged the other way and it roared in frustration. He was so close I felt the sound waves. I saw his pebbly-skinned throat vibrate. And worse, I saw into his mouth. A mouth glittering with teeth like butchers' knives and stained with the blood of his last kill.

I scrambled away again, stiff, barely able to move.

CRUNCH!

The Tyrannosaurus chomped its jaws shut on the tree itself. He began to twist and rip the tree, like a dog with a bone. Rending, tearing, bark flying, white wood pulp chewed to chips.

In a few seconds the tree would no longer be between us. And already I was too far morphed to run to another tree.

"Grrr-UNCH! Grrr-UNCH! Scree-EEEE-EEEE-crrUNCH! RrrrOOOAAAARRR!"

The Tyrannosaurus had gone mad with

frustration. It was screaming in rage, ripping, grinding, throwing its huge weight back and forth. Shaking the ground. Bruising the air with its insane roar. Just a few seconds more and . . .

Crrr-SNAP!

The tree fell slowly away, crashing down through layers of vines and ferns.

The Tyrannosaurus lunged, mouth open, red tongue lolling, teeth wet with drool.

I tried to leap back. I fell. Rolled. Thrashed, out of control.

Wings! I had wings!

Too late!

The mouth came down over me like some kind of earthmover, like a diesel shovel. A prison of teeth all round me. The jaw bit into the dirt itself. A root! Teeth snagged by a root. I flapped, ran, beat, rolled, scrambled.

Out between the jaws!

Running on osprey talons, running, wings open, flapping.

SNAP! Jaws a centimetre behind my tail.

Fly, fly, fly you idiot!

Bonk.

I never saw the tree trunk. I hit it head-on. I was stunned, senseless, helpless.

The Tyrannosaurus roared in triumph.

It towered above me, huge, irresistible. Pure

destruction. *Why had it chased me?* I wondered. Why? I was too small, wasn't I?

But of course. I'd been in predator morph before. I knew why. Because killing was what it did. Killing was what it was. It had gone beyond food or hunger now. It simply wanted to do what it did best.

I flapped weakly, too dazed to move.

Down came the head. Down from so far above. Down it came.

A swift movement to my right. What was it?

Fwapp! Fwapp! Fwapp!

An Andalite tail, too fast to be seen, struck three times.

The dinosaur swung its head hard. Ax went flying and rolled twice as he hit the ground.

The T-rex sagged. Tried to roar. And fell.

Human hands snatched me up as six tonnes of malevolence fell to the ground.

Chapter 11

 Ax

I wiped my tail blade on some large leaves. Unfortunately, more than my tail was stained.

My human friends were all looking at the big creature. Marco was becoming human again. I was busy trembling.

"Nice work, Ax," Prince Jake said. He slapped his hand on my shoulder. It is a thing humans do to indicate friendship or congratulations. Sometimes they do it to kill small insects called mosquitoes.

<I was toast,> Marco said, still more osprey than human. <You saved my life, man.>

<I was fortunate,> I said.

"I can't believe you took that monster down," Prince Jake said.

<Prince Jake, please don't think I can fight and defeat these creatures. This animal was busy chasing Marco. It was distracted. It is not accustomed to being attacked.>

"You're just being modest," Cassie said.

<No!> I said, more sharply than I'd intended. <Listen to me: I know my capabilities. In face-to-face, one-on-one combat, that creature would have destroyed me. One-against-one I will lose ninety per cent of the time.>

"Oh," Prince Jake said.

"Yeah, well, you came through big time on this go-round," Marco said. He held his hands out straight. They were trembling. "I can't stop shaking."

"This is insane," Cassie said. She looked around carefully. Peering cautiously, looking, no doubt, for others of the big creatures. "What is going on? Why are there dinosaurs here? Where is *here?*"

<Is there not some place on your planet where this creature lives?>

She shook her head violently. "No. Not in

millions of years, anyway. Tens of millions, probably. No, there is no place on Earth where tyrannosaurs just run around in the woods."

"Yeah, I think we'd have heard about it in school," Marco said. I believe his tone of voice indicated something the humans call "dry humour". I have not heard any wet humour, so it is difficult for me to tell the difference.

My immediate terror was fading. A deeper pessimism was setting in. It was easy to see that humans — or Andalites — deprived of the power of civilization were pathetically weak in this environment.

"Some kind of real-life *Jurassic Park*?" Prince Jake speculated. "Maybe someone actually did it. You know, cloned DNA from old dinosaur bones."

<That is scientifically possible,> I said. <But I have been feeling a strange distortion in my time-keeping sense. This planet is no longer rotating at the same speed as before. I think the likely explanation is that we have travelled a very, very long way in time.>

Prince Jake raised one eyebrow and looked at me. "Millions of years?"

<Once a *Sario Rip* — a time-rift — is created, there is no difference between a year and a million years. The energy required is the

same. I think I remember the equations . . . in an equation where t is time, z is Zero-space, w inversely cubed represents the nexus of—>

"Uh-uh," Marco said, raising his hand. "You saved my life. Don't undo it by killing me with algebra."

<I'm not an expert, of course. We studied the *Sario* effect in school. But I may not have been paying very close attention. Who knew I'd ever need to understand time-rifts?>

"How do we get back?" Cassie asked.

<I don't know. There is no way of duplicating the event that created the *Sario Rip*. That explosion in the submarine.>

"What? You can't just whip up a fusion bomb?" Marco said.

<Fusion bomb?> I asked. Then I laughed. I knew I shouldn't, but you have to admit, it was funny. <A *fusion* explosive? That's what it was? I assumed it was a small proton-shift weapon, at least. Fusion is only used in children's toys. You know, to make the little dolls speak and so on.>

My human friends stared at me.

"So the Andalite Toys 'R' Us must be a wild place, huh?" Marco said.

"Let's focus here," Prince Jake said impatiently. "Rachel and Tobias may have been killed. In any case, there's nothing we can do about it. We are millions of years in our own past, and there's nothing we can do about that. We're in the age of dinosaurs, and none of our morphs can even begin to fight things like. . ." He jerked his thumb at the massive corpse. ". . .like that. So the question is: what do we do?"

Prince Jake had summed up the situation very well. We were trapped in an exceedingly dangerous world where we could do almost nothing to defend ourselves.

I turned my stalk eyes towards the Tyrannosaurus's head. The mouth was partly open. The sight of those teeth made my insides watery all over again. I could see the serration on the back side of the teeth. Like shark teeth, only much, much bigger.

I had a clear mental picture of what would have happened if the creature had turned a little faster to confront me. The jaws closing over the upper half of my body . . . a violent shake of the head to rip me into easy-to-swallow pieces. . .

"We adapt," Cassie said grimly. "That's what animals have to do in order to survive. Our environment is massively different. No civilization to rely on, surrounded by brutal predators. So we adapt. Or we get eaten."

"Great. *Robinson Crusoe* meets *Jurassic*

Park. Look at us. We have nothing," Marco said. "No homes. No food. No tools. No weapons. We don't even have shoes!"

"Well, we're going to have to make all those things," Prince Jake said. "And we do have one big weapon: we can still morph. Maybe we can't fight a T-rex, but we can fly, and we can escape."

"We have food and shoes right here," Cassie said. She was looking at the dead Tyrannosaurus. "Ax has his tail. We can use the hide to make sandals. Skin from the lower leg there looks pretty tough and thick. We cut out some skin, remove the meat and eat it. Then we use ligaments and tendons to lace up the sandals."

I believe Prince Jake and Marco were shocked. Humans are strangely squeamish at times. I can never predict when.

"Wow," Marco said. "Wow. You're kind of getting into this, aren't you, Cassie?"

Cassie walked up to the dinosaur and placed one hand on its leg. She tested the skin with her fingertips. "Look, Marco, my best friend is gone. Tobias is gone. I don't want any more names added to that list. We need food. There's no Burger King anywhere nearby, OK? We're not big or mean enough to be predators in this environment. We've moved way down on the food chain. The best we can be is scavengers. Here's thousands of kilogrammes of protein. We eat some now, and we smoke some for jerky so we can eat later."

If anything, Prince Jake and Marco appeared even more shocked. And I felt the same. This was an aspect of Cassie I'd never seen. But then, Cassie is more involved than the others in the facts of environment. She had sized up the situation and realized that in this new world she and her fellow humans were no longer masters.

I began to feel a little better about our chances. Humans may be technologically primitive, not to mention physically weak, what with tottering around on two spindly legs. But if you're in a situation that requires instant adaptability to change, you should always have a couple of humans along with you.

Cassie looked at me, making eye contact with my main eyes. "Ax, are you OK doing this? Your tail is all we have."

<Yes. I will do all I can.>

"OK, then. Jake, maybe you and Marco could gather up any dry sticks and dry grass you can find nearby. We have to work fast. We aren't the only animals who'll be after this much meat. Ax? I need you to slice this area of leg into squares, each about thirty centimetres square."

I glanced at Prince Jake.

Prince Jake smiled and shrugged. "Cassie's the boss on this," he said. "She has a clue. I don't. And we all know Marco doesn't."

"You got that right," Marco agreed.

I turned all my eyes on the haunch of the dead creature. I took careful aim and began the work.

Chapter 12

 Rachel

My feet were torn bloody. I was leaving traces of red on the razor-edged saw grass. The legs of my leotard were torn and tattered. It was not a good look. The bare midriff thing, maybe. The fringe look? No.

I was carrying Tobias in my arms. He couldn't fly. He was too slow at walking. And if I carried him perched on my shoulder, no matter how careful he was, the jerking and wobbling would force him to dig his talons into my skin.

Not fun. Especially not fun because the whole time I was expecting some murderous dinosaur to come ripping out of the woods to our left.

<You doing OK?> Tobias asked.

"Sure. No problem," I said, trying to sound cheerful. "I could stand a little less humidity, maybe."

<Yes, it is . . . unh . . . damp.>

His groan of pain made me feel guilty for thinking about my own problems. "Tobias, maybe you should morph to human for a while."

<I'm sorry. You must be getting tired of carrying me.>

"No, no, it's not that. It's just that your wing is hurting you. If you were in human morph, there wouldn't be any pain."

<I can only stay in morph for two hours, Rachel. Then I have to demorph and I'm right back where I started. Plus I won't continue healing during that time. Not to mention the fact you'd have to redo my splint. And that wasn't fun for either of us.>

"You could just stay human. Permanently. There are worse things."

He didn't say anything for a while. When he did speak, it wasn't about morphing. <Can you lift me up for a minute? I think I see something.>

I raised him up high above my head. "What is it?"

<Smoke! I see a column of smoke.>

"Like a forest fire? Or is it that volcano?"

<No, like a camp-fire!>

I lowered him back down. "Maybe it's the others. Maybe they made it to shore and started a fire. I mean, there are no humans here, right?"

<Not for another sixty or eighty million years,> Tobias said. <Not even monkeys. Not even our most distant relatives. The only mammals around are early versions of rats and shrews.>

I smiled. "If Marco were here he'd make some snide remark about you having plenty to eat, at least."

Tobias laughed. <Yeah. And speaking of which. . .>

"At least we have water as long as we stay by the river. On the other hand, what if that smoke is from Cassie and Jake? We have to go find out. Besides, the sun's going down. We could use a fire."

<You go,> Tobias said. <It looks like it's about two or three kilometres away. You could morph to your bald eagle body, fly over, take a look, and come right back for me.>

"Yeah, right. Like I'm going to leave you here in the middle of nowhere, helpless."

He argued with me a little. Said he'd be OK and so on. But there was no way. We decided to drink our fill from the river. Then we turned away from it towards the smoke. Already it was harder to see in the fading sunlight.

The saw grass gradually gave way to shorter grasses. And the forest that had been on our left the whole time receded. We were walking now across a plain that looked like something you'd expect to see lions roaming. But we were tens of millions of years away from lions.

"Lions I could handle," I muttered.

<What?>

"Nothing. Just thinking out loud. Oh, man!"

<What?>

"I have to set you down for a second," I said. I laid him back on the golden, half-metre-high grass. I began to pick the insects off my feet. Several different species of bugs had been attracted to the cuts on my feet.

<Rachel, why didn't you tell me your feet looked like that?> Tobias cried.

I shrugged. "Looks worse than it is. Besides, this grass we're in now isn't bad."

<You have to take it easy for a while, Rachel. You're going to end up as—>

He fell silent. He cocked his hawk's head left, then right.

"What is it?"

<I hear something. Something large.>

In addition to their amazing sense of sight, birds of prey also hear very, very well. I jumped up, grabbed him, and held him high over my head to give him the best possible view. But the truth is, I could see what there was to see well enough.

I almost dropped him.

Four . . . no five creatures that looked a little like rhinoceroses. Only instead of one horn, they had two hugely long horns protruding from a thick, scalloped shell around their heads.

"Even I know that dinosaur," I said. "Those are Triceratops. But they're just plant-eaters, right? Not dangerous?"

<No, they aren't dangerous,> Tobias agreed. <But what you can't see is the pack of Deinonychus moving in to attack them. *They're* dangerous. But I don't think there are enough of them to go after a Triceratops. The Tri's can make a run for the river, get their backs to it, and the Deinonychus would be out of luck.>

I didn't ask how Tobias could size up the situation so well. Probably because he is a predator. Actually, two kinds of predator: hawk and human. The combination of hawk instincts and human intelligence gives him a lot of insight into the battle for survival.

<Strange. Deinonychus was supposed to have been a smart pack-hunter. But these guys have blown it. Unless. . .>

He turned his head to look behind us and let out a thought-speak moan.

<Score one for Deinonychus. We've screwed up,> he said. <They're behind us. Coming slowly this way in a pincer action to trap the Triceratops.>

"How big do you think they are?"

<Not big. Maybe a metre and a half tall, three metres long from nose to tail.>

"Big deal. That's only about the size of a big kid or a small man."

<Wrong comparison. That's about the size of a wolf. We're talking very fast, very smart wolves.>

They were close enough now that I could see them, even with my sun-strained human eyes. Man-sized lizards bounding along on powerful legs. Their pebbly skin was the colour of asparagus soup and coffee ice cream, swirled together. Not that I was getting really hungry or anything.

A gust of wind ruffled my hair. The wind blew our scent towards the Deinonychus. I saw one of them stop, raise his head, and turn it towards us.

I felt the eyes searching for me. And I swear I felt the moment when those cold, yellow eyes locked onto me.

"Hroooo! Hroooo!" the dinosaur cried.

They broke into a run.

"Uh-oh." I grabbed Tobias and started to run, the pain in my bloody feet forgotten. Stupid. I might as well have been trying to outrun a wolf.

<The other pack is coming after us, too!> Tobias yelled.

Suddenly it wasn't the big Triceratops caught in the Deinonychus's trap. It was a much, much easier prey.

Chapter 13

 Cassie

"Faster . . . OK, more grass . . . OK, hoooof, hoooof!"

I blew lightly on the dry grass. Jake moved the tendon bow back and forth as fast as he could. Marco held the top of the stick.

It had taken a while for us to piece together old bits of forgotten Boy Scout lore and scenes we'd seen on TV or in movies or read about in books.

But eventually we'd figured it out, starting

with a flat piece of wood as a base. Ax cut a small notch in it. We then took a straight stick about thirty centimetres long. That we held upright, using pieces of bark to protect the holder's hands from the friction.

We fashioned a bow by stringing a length of Tyrannosaurus tendon cut from the animal's foot. We put a half loop of the bowstring around the upright stick. Then all we had to do was move the bow quickly back and forth. The vertical stick spun in the groove of the flat base piece. And slowly but surely, the heat of friction began to glow.

I grabbed a tiny handful of dry grass. I bent over, my face just centimetres away from the base. I added a bit more grass and blew again, gently, gently.

A piece of grass crisped and twisted. More air. I blew harder. More browning, twisting grass. I began to despair.

"Flame!" Marco cried.

It was true. A tiny flame. Very tiny. I fed more grass into it. More grass. Now the tiniest twigs. The twig caught fire!

I looked up at Jake and Marco. Their faces were shining.

"Wow," I whispered. "This is the first deliberately made fire. Ever. We just invented fire."

Ax leaned down low to help pile larger sticks on the flame. It was mesmerizing. The flame grew and grew. It ate up the grass and moved up to the sticks.

I just sat there, feeling weird and significant and yet silly. It was like a holy religious ritual. Man creating fire.

Or in this case, woman, I thought with a grin. Rachel will appreciate. . . But no, Rachel wasn't around any more.

Marco stepped away and came back with a long stick. He'd impaled a half dozen shreds of Tyrannosaurus meat on the stick. He held them over the fire.

They crackled and sizzled and smelled wonderful.

I folded my legs and my awkward Tyrannosaurus sandals under me. It was starting to get dark under the trees. But we had fire. We alone, on all of planet Earth, had fire.

We had moved away from the dead dinosaur just as a bunch of very tiny, swift, two-legged dinosaurs showed up looking for a late lunch. We were now camped at the edge of the plain, with the woods fifty metres away at our backs. We'd chosen the spot because there was a stream running by. And because we just didn't know which was safer: open country or woods.

"OK, who's going to be first?" Marco asked, holding out a strip of hot meat. "We have medium rare and well-done."

Jake reached for the slice. He took a cautious bite.

"Just don't say it tastes like chicken," Marco said.

Jake considered. "It tastes like fish, actually. Like a mild fish. Maybe like swordfish. It could use some salt."

Marco cocked an eyebrow at me. "Now he's a food expert?"

I laughed softly. I took a piece. It was delicious. But then again, I was starving.

"The first cooked food in all of history," Marco observed. "Plus the first complaint about food in all of history. Ax-man, you want to grind a hoof into a piece of this? Or maybe you could morph to human and eat it?"

Andalites eat by absorbing grass through their hooves as they run or walk.

<No, thanks. I've grazed very well.>

Ax was watching the grassy plain. He was using his stalk eyes to swivel carefully in all directions.

The sky was shading from blue to brilliant red and orange, with sunset coming on quickly. A massive, distorted-looking red sun slipped below a layer of high clouds and dropped behind the volcano.

"Beautiful," I said, mostly to myself.

"The first person in history to appreciate a sunset," Marco said.

"How much longer do you figure you'll be doing that, Marco?" Jake asked tolerantly.

Marco grinned. His face was red from the glow of sunset. "The first person to ever complain about someone talking too much."

"What are we going to do about it getting dark?" I asked.

Jake looked surprised. "I don't know. You've been so cool about all this back-to-nature stuff, I guess I was waiting for you to tell us."

Was he resentful that I had been taking a more active role? No. Surely not. "I don't have any brilliant ideas."

"Doesn't fire keep animals away?" Marco asked.

"Not always," I said. "Not predators. In Africa, man-eating lions and leopards go right to villages, into huts and drag people away. In grasslands like this, you get lightning fires all the time. Some of the predators may have learned to let the fire drive smaller prey towards them."

"The first really, really depressing example

of way too much information in all of history," Marco said.

"We have our weapons," I said.

Jake said, "Yeah. Three sharp sticks. Plus Ax's tail. Throw in some burning torches and we can probably handle some of the smaller predators."

I felt a chill and scooted closer to the fire, which now blazed up fairly well. The image of a huge T-rex looming up suddenly, gold and red from the firelight, its vast mouth open, eyes greedy . . . I took a couple of deep breaths.

I'm not Rachel. I can't just turn off the fear. If Rachel were here, she'd say something cocky about kicking Tyrannosaurus butt. We'd all know it was just bold talk, but we'd feel better, anyway.

"OK," Jake said. "We sleep in shifts. Ax's time-tracking sense is messed up, but he can approximate two hours and wake us up. Two of us awake at all times. The people who are awake will sit facing out, away from the fire. That way their eyes will be adjusted to seeing in the dark."

"Good plan," Marco said. "That way there'll be two of us to scream, 'Oh no, we're toast!' when the next Big Rex shows up."

"If a predator shows up, what do we do?" I asked.

Jake considered for a moment. "I think the most dangerous morph any of us has is my tiger morph. If we're attacked, I'll morph. Ax will use his tail. Cassie and Marco, you grab your weapons. The three of you try and hold off the . . . the whatever shows up . . . till I've morphed. An Andalite and a tiger together should be enough. Then Marco and Cassie, you two will morph. But morph something to escape, not fight."

"Cassie and I, we wave sharp sticks at a Big Rex?" Marco asked sceptically. "Meanwhile, you're helpless in mid-morph."

"You have a better plan?" Jake asked testily.

"Sure. If Big Mister T shows up, we scream and cry and blubber like babies till he eats us."

Jake grinned. Then he laughed. So did I. It wasn't even slightly funny, of course, but sometimes fear and exhaustion can combine to make you giddy.

"OK, Cassie and Ax take the first watch. Marco, you and I have to try and sleep."

"At least I won't have any bad dreams," Marco said. "I'm already in one."

Jake and Marco fell silent. I don't know if they slept at all. I turned away from the fire and looked out into darkness that was deepening with shocking speed. Already the night was rushing towards us out of the east, pushing away the last tendrils of red sunlight.

Then I saw it. Like someone had painted a brush stroke of fairy dust across the sky.

"Ax," I whispered. "Is that a comet?"

<Yes. It is very beautiful.>

"Even to you? You must have seen comets up in space."

<They are most beautiful when they are closest to a star. The star, the sun, is what causes the tail to extend.>

"Oh. Looks close."

<It may be,> Ax said. <It is either very close or very large. My people — a long time ago, of course — used to believe that comets were omens of bad things that would happen.>

I was surprised. "Really? Humans thought the same thing." Darkness fell. There was no moon in the sky. The starlight never touched the grass sea around us. The firelight was puny.

"Are you scared, Ax?"

<Yes.>

"Me, too."

I felt the stick in my hand. I felt the fire at my back. Little, weak, defenceless Homo sapiens, I faced a night full of terrors.

Chapter 14

 Tobias

Deinonychus. That's what they were, I was pretty sure. At least, I thought so. I couldn't remember. But learning about dinosaurs in books isn't like seeing them face-to-face.

They were hunting us. Like a wolf pack. They were taking their time because we were unfamiliar prey. A strange creature that ran on two legs while carrying a big bird.

Yes, we were something new. New meat.

Rachel ran towards the spot where the

camp-fire had been before the failing light had rendered the smoke invisible. It had seemed to be coming from the edge of the plain that opened before us. As she ran, I watched the Deinonychus pack. I watched them as a professional predator myself.

Was there communication between them? It sure seemed like the two bands of Deinonychus were moving in concert.

It was a triangle, basically. One group behind and to the west. The second group level with us but to the east. We were running north. If we veered slightly left, we'd hit the edge of the forest. Was that the right move?

<Rachel, head for the woods.>

"Why?" she managed to gasp. Rachel's in shape, but running barefoot while carrying a hawk is not easy.

<They're pack-hunters. I think the two groups can see each other and adjust to each other. Even in this light. In the trees they'll lose their line of sight.>

Rachel didn't say anything. But she did veer left a little. Towards the trees.

I focused my hawk eyes on the westerly group. They were speeding up!

A quick glance to the east. They were speeding up, too, but only after the first group did.

<I thought so,> I said. <The leader of the pack is with that western bunch. I think I know which one it is. He's got about half a metre of his tail missing.>

The Deinonychus were running now. They were quite fast. And so close I could see details of the leader: the pebbly lizard skin, the way the tail stuck out stiff as a board for balance, the placid expression on that intelligent face.

His weapons were formidable. He stood no taller than a short man or a tall boy. But his jaw could close over a human head. His hands were relatively larger and stronger than a Tyrannosaurus's, with wicked, down-curved claws. But it was the feet that were the main weapon. They were talons, not so very different from my own. But on each foot there was an upraised claw, maybe twenty centimetres long. It reminded me of Ax's tail blade. That claw, kicked by that coiled steel leg, would slice through a car door.

<We'll reach the woods before them,> I said. <But then we have to act quickly. We have to separate.>

"No way!"

She assumed I was being self-sacrificing. <Rachel, look. They're after *you*, not me. I have a plan.>

She said nothing. Just gasped and panted. I

could hear her heart pounding madly.

Trees! We hit the tree line and suddenly it occurred to me just how late in the day it was. The sun was setting in a blaze of glory out on the plain, but under the trees it was already night.

<Stop right here.>

Rachel stopped. She dropped me in the dead leaves. She bent over double, hands on her knees, throwing up from exhaustion. The predator in me was glad. Perfect. The powerful, unfamiliar scent would draw the Deinonychus right to this point.

<OK, I can't fly, but I can grip. I want you to throw me. Straight up. Up into this tree. Up to that branch.>

"Wha . . . wha. . ."

<Rachel, don't argue. Throw me. Then run and do your bear morph. It may buy you time.>

Besides, I added silently, *you don't want to die as helpless prey. As a human, you'll simply be ripped apart. You'll be eaten alive. As a bear, they'll at least have to fight you first.*

Rachel stood up. Then she bent over, cramped in her right side. She winced in pain. I could see her feet were torn. She was exhausted. But not beaten yet. When she met my gaze, I still saw fierce Rachel in her blue eyes.

<We have to do this now,> I said. <They'll be here in less than a minute.>

"OK." She reached down and lifted me up. Like someone heaving a basketball from her chest, she threw me upward. Too low! I missed the branch. I flapped my wings, an instinct. A painful, searingly painful, instinct. I hit the ground.

"I can't do it."

<Do it!>

She grabbed me again. This time she put her whole body into it. Up! The branch. I flapped my good wing, spun in the air, grabbed. Yes. I grabbed with my second talon and held firm.

<Now, run! Run!>

She ran. At least, she hobbled and staggered away through the trees. And I waited. I waited and tried not to think of what would happen to Rachel if I messed up.

My branch was just two metres above the ground. I felt totally helpless. I was a bird who could not fly. And there is nothing weaker than a bird who can't fly.

I gripped my branch. Noises. Many clawed feet running. A Deinonychus appeared. Its tail was minus about thirty centimetres of length. The leader of the pack.

"Heeeeessss!"

He froze. He looked at the mess Rachel had left. But he did not walk under my branch. Then another Deinonychus. This one ran right over and sniffed curiously. He had a jagged scar sixty centimetres long down his back. I could see it clearly.

Short-tail turned away. Scar walked beneath me. His head was just thirty centimetres below me.

Now!

I dropped. I opened my talons. I sank them into reptilian skin, right along the old scar.

"Hrroooohhh!"

The Deinonychus turned his head to glare at me with one eye. He opened a mouth lined with ridiculously large teeth.

I almost lost it. I had to fight the urge to flap away, broken wing and all.

Focus, Tobias, I told myself. I locked the fear out of my mind. I held tight with my talons. And I focused on the dinosaur.

It may have been sixty-five or seventy or eighty million years B.C., but DNA was still DNA.

Chapter 15

 Tobias

I acquired the Deinonychus. I absorbed his DNA into me. And he grew passive and calm, like most animals do when being acquired.

When I was done he wandered away, as if he'd forgotten what he'd been doing.

I stood there, utterly vulnerable on the forest floor. And then I heard a roar. Not a saurian roar, but the full-throated roar of a very large mammal.

Rachel!

I focused my mind again. I pictured the

Deinonychus in my mind. And slowly at first, then faster, the changes began.

All right, Tobias, keep your mind strong! I warned myself. It was a new morph. I'd have to deal with the Deinonychus's instincts.

My feathers began to stiffen and harden. It was as if someone were coating them with rubber cement or something. The feather pattern remained at first, but they were glued down. And then they began to melt together.

My beak began to extend, out and out, and at the same time the edges became serrated, almost like a saw. And each saw tooth grew and extended, longer and longer, to begin to form the teeth of the Deinonychus.

All the while I grew. Up and up. From standing thirty centimetres tall to five times that height.

My tail feathers twined and twisted together and then my tail hardened and grew. Out and out, impossibly long!

Everywhere I could feel the muscles bulging and growing. Layers of muscle over thickening bones. I rose high on legs like steel springs. My talons became less graceful and more deadly. I found I could raise the huge, killing claw. Yes, that's how I would run, with that claw raised so that nothing would dull its razor-sharpness.

I loved that claw. I pictured it ripping open . . . no! Already the dinosaur's instincts were struggling to rise up in my own mind.

But that wasn't going to happen. It *couldn't* happen. Rachel needed me.

But the power! The vivid, electric energy in every cell of my body!

My eyesight grew dim. But not much worse than human eyes, and better in that they could see fairly well in the dark. My hearing diminished, but again, not by much. And to compensate for those losses, the sense of smell flooded my consciousness.

What?

What smell was that?

I stood up and sniffed the wind.

"Roooooaaarrrr!" a deep, hoarse voice bellowed.

"Heeeesss! Heeeesss!" A more familiar cry.

The hunt was on! The pack had cornered its prey. I had to hurry. Hurry, or all the best meat would be taken. I'd have nothing but cold carrion.

With my mouth watering, I bounded away, tearing through the underbrush to join the pack.

Chapter 16

 Jake

I woke up. It was dark. I was all hot on the side near the fire and cold on the other side. I heard the gurgling of the stream. I'd been dreaming of home. In my dream I was eating dinosaur-shaped cereal at the breakfast table with my parents.

I didn't want to think about my parents. What they would be going through worrying about me just made me sick to my stomach.

"Have you seen anything?"

"Yaaahhh!" Cassie yelped. Then, "Good grief, you scared me."

Marco moaned in his sleep.

I rubbed my eyes. I could not believe I had actually fallen asleep. But obviously I had. "Ax, how are you doing?"

<I am well. My time-sense has returned fully. It takes a while to calibrate for the rotation of a planet. This planet rotates differently than it does in our own time.>

"How long was I asleep?"

<Approximately one of the current hours and fifty-two minutes.> He came close and tossed another piece of wood on the fire.

I stretched out my foot and poked Marco. He moaned again. Then he sat up. "Oh. So it wasn't a dream. Too bad."

"Cassie, you and Ax can—" I stopped. I had looked up at the sky. "What is that?"

"It's a comet," Cassie said. "Isn't it absolutely beautiful?"

"Yeah. Looks awfully close." I gazed up at the sweep of bright dust trailing from the brilliant head.

<It is. In the last three hours it has grown noticeably larger.>

I glanced over at Ax. He was outlined against the stars, a dark shadow with stalk eyes turning restlessly. "It's not going to hit us or anything, is it?" I laughed when I said it.

<I don't think so. First of all, the odds against any particular comet hitting a particular planet are very large. Millions to one at the very least. Especially since Earth is not large enough to exert much of a gravitational pull. Besides, the comet is now so close and moving so quickly, I have been able to keep track of a rough trajectory. It will be very close. No more than one or two diameters of Earth, perhaps. But I believe it will miss.>

"Well, that's a relief," Marco said. "I wouldn't want to get killed by a comet and cheat the dinosaurs out of eating me."

"You two get some sleep," I said to Ax and Cassie. "Marco and I will take over. But actually, first I have to . . . um . . . I have to take a little walk."

I left the cosy glow of the fire and headed into darkness. Seven metres, and the fire already seemed like part of some different world. It was so dark. I looked back and it was as if the fire and the comet were both floating in the same empty space.

I did what I had to do, then I saw it. A flash! A sudden flash of light. Low on the horizon to the north. Was it a meteorite? A falling star?

99

No. There it was again. Faint. A tiny stab of red light. Again. Again.

I hurried back to the others. "Look to the north. Do you guys—"

A flash like the sun exploding! High overhead.

The flash lit up the entire landscape for just an instant. But in that instant I saw them: a herd of vast creatures. They stood on four tree-trunk legs. They had tremendously long necks and tails that were just as long. It was impossible to know their actual size, but they had to stand at least four or five times my own height. And from head to tail they had to be fourteen metres.

I'd seen at least ten of them moving towards us along the line of the stream.

And in that same flash of light, the huge dinosaurs had seen something, too. Coming up behind them, on their trail, like a monster in the night, a Tyrannosaurus.

Boom! Boom! Boom! Boom!

The big dinosaurs bolted, breaking into a panicked run. Straight for our camp!

"What was that flash?" Cassie cried as I ran for the fire.

"Everybody run!" I yelled. "It's a stampede."

"Stampede? What is this, a cowboy movie?!" Marco demanded incredulously.

"MOVE!"

Boom! Boom! Boom! BOOM! BOOM! BOOM!

It was like the worst thunderstorm in history. Creatures five times the size of elephants were stampeding. Every step of those big feet was like a pile driver.

"Get across the stream!" I yelled.

"Where is it?"

"What stream?"

"Just follow me."

I ran, making sure Cassie and Marco were keeping up. Ax, I didn't have to worry about. He was far faster than any of us.

The thunder grew louder. All around us. I saw a vast bulk beside me, blocking out the stars. The panicked herd was all around us.

"HRRRROOOOOAAAARRRR!"

My knees turned to jelly. I tripped. I hit hard. The wind was knocked out of me.

A massive, taloned foot landed centimetres from my head. I rolled. I slammed into a tree trunk. No, the leg of the long-necked dinosaur.

"ScreeeEEEEE!" the terrified animal cried as the Tyrannosaurus bent low. I saw teeth glittering in moonlight. I saw a glowing yellow eye. I heard the chomp of the Tyrannosaurus's jaws as they clamped down.

I was beneath the long-necked dinosaur as it

fought. If I'd stood up and stretched, I would have just reached its belly. Tree-trunk legs pounded around me in a frenzy. And all the while the two animals roared and screamed and bellowed in terror and rage.

I covered my ears and screamed. A battle of giants right above me. I couldn't see anything but darkness blotting out stars and the faintest outline of a creature the size of a whale.

I was a cockroach being hunted with sledge-hammers. The ground jumped and slammed into me with each impact. I couldn't even see the legs scuffling and pounding. At any second one would crush me. I curled up in a ball and tucked my head down and shook.

What morph did I have to fight these titans? Nothing. This wasn't my world. I was nothing in this world. All my powerful morphs were nothing in this world.

"ScreeeEEEEEE-uh. ScreeeEEEEE-uh!"

"Huh-huh-RoooAAAARRRR!"

A final cry of the big dinosaur ended in a gasp and a collapsing rattle.

The Tyrannosaurus had won. The long-necked dinosaur was done for. Nothing left but for him to fall. Nothing left but for him to drop down on to me.

Chapter 17

 Rachel

They were around me. All around me. Maybe ten of them. Deinonychus, Tobias had called them. Like wolves. They circled me like wolves.

They were not big, certainly smaller than my grizzly bear morph. Maybe three metres from half-grinning mouth to rigid tail. But they were dangerous. Even with my dim grizzly bear eyesight, I could see their bristling weapons. The scythe-clawed hands; the huge ripping talon; the razor-sharp teeth.

I had weapons of my own. I had strength enough in my arms and shoulders to push over a Toyota. I had my own evil, ripping claws. I had teeth. But I was not fooled. I knew my only hope was that the Deinonychus would be discouraged by the fact that I was unknown prey.

Maybe the pack could be scared off. Maybe they wouldn't like the smell of bear. I wondered if Tobias was safe up in his tree. I hoped so.

The leader, the Deinonychus with the shortened tail, stepped to the front.

"HhhooorrRAAWWWRR!" I roared, and rose up erect to my impressive two-plus metres. In my own time, there was no land predator as large or with as much raw power as a grizzly. But this was a whole different time. And a way, way different standard of large.

I knew these Deinonychus shared an environment with Tyrannosaurus and probably a dozen other very big, very dangerous lizards. And they thrived in that environment. How was I ever going to scare them?

The leader cocked his head and listened to me roar. He looked directly at me, considering, wondering.

Then two of them leaped!

"RROOAAARRR!" I bellowed. I swung my meat-hook claw with all my might. It was a lucky blow. I caught the closest Deinonychus across the neck. He collapsed.

With no signal that I could see, they all backed away. The leader sniffed at me. He sniffed at his comrade, who was no longer moving. Intelligent eyes considered.

This time I heard a signal. It was almost the cheeping of a songbird. "Neep!"

The Deinonychus pack circled around. It was so precise. So planned, almost rehearsed. They were not running away. They were not giving up. Instead they were preparing a more concerted attack.

They were prepared to take losses. That meant they would press the attack this time. Press the attack till I was down. Till I was food.

But something wasn't right. I could see it in the leader's eyes. He was glaring hard at a Deinonychus that had just arrived.

This new dinosaur stepped forward. He sniffed at me from a safe distance. And then, without warning, he leaped!

A slash with his left foot claw ripped a sixty-centimetre-long slice in my chest. It hadn't cut deep into vital organs but it hurt.

"HhhhRROOOAAARRR!" I bellowed.

But there was an even louder roar. The leader of the pack screamed at the impertinent new dinosaur. The new Deinonychus jumped back, away from me, and spun around to face the enraged pack leader.

The two Deinonychus stood bristling, face-to-face. A challenge! That was it. The new Deinonychus had ignored the leader. He'd attacked on his own. And that was an attack on the leader's dominance.

The leader hissed. It was a low, sinister sound. He stuck his tail straight back. The challenger raised his clawed hands, ready for battle.

And it was only then that I spotted the twisted pieces of fabric around the challenger's arm. Fabric torn from my own leotard and wrapped around Tobias's splint.

<Tobias!> I cried. It *was* Tobias. It had to be. But he had ripped a hole in me. . .

I realized what had happened. Tobias had somehow acquired this Deinonychus's DNA and morphed him. But in doing so he'd lost control. The Deinonychus's instincts had pushed Tobias's mind aside and taken control.

And now Tobias was in a showdown with the pack leader. A showdown to determine who would be boss. And who would be in charge of destroying me.

Tobias and the leader circled each other slowly, warily.

<Tobias! Listen to me. You've morphed a dinosaur. You've lost control. It happens sometimes. You need to—>

The pack leader leaped! He landed, deadly feet out, mouth snapping, right where Tobias had been a split second before. But Tobias had dodged left, then crouched low to get in under the leader's guard.

Chomp!

"ScrrEEEEE!"

The leader jumped back, shocked. A piece of his left flank was missing.

Tobias circled again, tail stiff as a pole behind him.

Now the leader was more cautious. He waited for Tobias to make the first move. It wasn't a long wait. Tobias charged. With split-second timing, the other dinosaur jumped up in the air. He met Tobias's face with his own wicked talons.

Slash!

"ScrrrEEEE-uh!" Tobias fell back. Blood gushed from a wound in his face. The pack leader pressed the attack. Tobias stumbled back in seeming panic.

"Hrrooo-HAH!" A cry of triumph came from the pack leader. He leaped.

Too soon! Tobias was under him, ripping

upward with his forepaws. He jammed his claws into the other Deinonychus's chest.

The pack leader screamed and flailed. But he could not tear Tobias's teeth away from him. It was over.

Tobias stood up. And he screeched a loud cry of challenge.

"Hreee-YAH! Hreee-hrEEEE-YAH!"

He looked at the rest of the pack. They looked at their fallen leader. Then they looked at Tobias. And one by one, like vanquished knights offering their swords to the victor, they each lowered their noses to the ground in submission.

Tobias turned. Turned to look at me.

<Tobias, it's me, Rachel. Listen to me, it's Rachel.>

I was using one paw to hold my own wound closed. The pain was intense. But the fear was greater. I saw the look in Tobias's eyes.

<Tobias, you are human. You are human. Get control of the morph!>

He advanced towards me. He was hungry. The others advanced just a step behind him.

<Tobias! Listen to me. You are a human being! It's me, Rachel. Your friend. You are human, you. . .>

No, I realized. No, that was wrong, wasn't it?

<Tobias. You are a *hawk*. You are a red-tailed

108

hawk. Remember your wings? Remember flying? Flying high on the thermals?>

His deadly jaw was centimetres away. He stopped. He tilted his head. And suddenly, his entire body seemed to shudder.

<Rachel?> he said.

Chapter 18

 Jake

Down it came. Like having the Goodyear blimp dropped on top of you. Only much, much heavier.

I couldn't see a thing, only feel the air rush aside as the beast fell. I rolled.

WHUUUUUMP!

"Aaaahhh!" I cried. I was pinned. My legs were caught beneath the long-necked dinosaur's belly. Just my lower legs, and nothing had been broken, but when I tried to move I realized I was trapped.

"Jake!" Cassie cried. "Where are you?"

I wanted to tell her to shut up and save herself. Another part of me wanted to beg her to help me.

I was shaking. Literally shaking. Like I had fever chills and I just couldn't stop them.

CHOMP!

The huge head came down and ripped violently into the long-necked dinosaur.

CHOMP!

The Tyrannosaurus was eating ravenously. Just a metre or so above my head. Then I guess it chomped into something tough, because it yanked. And that yanking lifted the big dinosaur's weight off me for a second.

I was out!

I rolled. I jumped to my feet.

"Ooof!" I went down. My legs had gone numb from being pinned. I could move them, but—

Down it came! Flashing teeth all around me. No way out. I curled into a ball.

"Oh, God!" I cried.

The Tyrannosaurus's jaw closed around me. I clenched my arms and legs tight together. Still those teeth cut grooves in my left shoulder. No room! The mouth was too narrow. I pushed my numb legs out before me, down the Tyrannosaurus's throat.

I was in the Tyrannosaurus's mouth. No room to move. Stinking foul air. Sticky saliva all over me. A big tongue that tried to push the rest of me down the waiting, greedy throat. He closed his mouth and crushed the air out of my lungs.

I grabbed that tongue. I locked my fingers on the rough, wet thing and focused with all that was left of my terrified, jibbering brain.

I wasn't even sure I'd acquired the DNA when I started trying to morph. I was doing it all at once. I was acquiring and morphing and screaming in terror.

But I began to grow. I couldn't be near those teeth when I grew. They would lacerate me. I wormed down the roaring Tyrannosaurus's throat. Down away from the teeth. Its powerful throat muscles were pummelling my legs now, but I was morphing.

The Tyrannosaurus realized something was wrong. It had swallowed the wrong thing. It coughed and gagged. Then, a massive surge of muscle spasm, and I was falling.

Flump!

I hit the soft side of the fallen long-necked dinosaur. I tried to grab on, but failed. My hands weren't my hands any more.

I rolled onto the ground at the Tyrannosaurus's feet. I was at his mercy. Utterly.

But the big monster was not able to attack. Something had happened to its insides. I don't know if I ruptured something, or what. But the tyrant lizard stomped three, four, five steps away and collapsed. It sat down on its tail, then fell over on to its side, moaning.

I lay there gasping, not knowing what body I had, not caring. I was alive. I tried my mouth. No, I couldn't talk. I demorphed. Then tried again.

"Cassie! Marco! Ax!"

"Jake?" Cassie's voice cried in the darkness.

It took a few seconds for us to find each other back at the glowing embers of the campfire. Cassie put her arms around me, slime and all, and hugged me. I was too shaky to return the hug, but it felt good.

"Is it dead?" Marco asked.

"No," I said. "But I think I hurt it. It's on its side over there, I think."

"You know what we should do," Marco said grimly. "We should all acquire that Tyrannosaurus. We need one alive to acquire. It's alive. Until we acquire a Big Rex we're just going to get chased around until sooner or later we get eaten."

"I already did it," I said. "But you're right."

None of them were anxious to walk over and

start touching that creature. Even moaning on its side, it was terrifying.

We came up slowly, carefully, tentatively beneath the tail. We carried small torches to light our way.

Marco was the first. He pressed his hand against the crocodile-like flesh.

And then Ax.

And lastly Cassie.

It was strange. Like some kind of ritual. Three humans and an alien, all carrying torches that might as well have been cinders in the endless darkness. We cowered before the groaning, wheezing monster and touched it.

"It's so strange," Cassie said. "We're humans in a time millions of years before the first humans. In our time, Homo sapiens run the planet. In this time it's the Tyrannosaurus. You always wonder who would have won, if humans and dinosaurs had lived at the same time. Who would have survived?"

"They would have hunted us like cats hunt mice," Marco said. "Primitive humans with sharp sticks and maybe a couple of torches? No contest."

<Yes, but you are not just *primitive* humans,> Ax said. <You are primitive humans with Andalite morphing technology.>

Not for the first time, I wondered if Ax had developed a sense of humour.

And then the adrenalin and lack of sleep and the physical beating all came together. My eyes closed all on their own. My legs buckled. I fell, and arms reached out to take me.

Chapter 19

 Marco

After we let Jake sort of doze for a while, we decided that maybe sleeping between a dead long-necked dinosaur the size of Nebraska and a moaning, sick Tyrannosaurus was not a great idea.

So despite the fact that it was so dark we couldn't see our own feet, we trudged on. At least it wasn't raining. After that big huge flash, I'd assumed rain was coming. But maybe that's not the way it worked in this millennium.

"So basically everything is fine," I said, shifting my pathetically dim torch to my other hand. "We're tens of millions of years in the past. We have no food except charred scraps of dinosaur-on-a-stick. There's a river over there, but if we do go and get a drink, some monster crocodile will jump out and chomp us. We're lost, which is fine because let's face it, we're not exactly looking for the nearest Taco Bell, so who cares where we are? Plus, just to make things perfect, we're wearing Tyrannosaurus skin sandals, which is going to really, really endear us to the next Big Rex we see."

"I wish Rachel were here," Cassie said.

"Yeah," I said, suddenly sad. "She'd say something like, 'I can stand the dinosaurs, Marco, I just can't stand listening to you whine'."

Jake laughed softly. "You do a pretty good Rachel impression."

I heard Cassie sniffle.

"You know what occurs to me," I said. "We survived, right? I mean, twice we've been jumped by tyrannosaurs or tyrannosauri, whichever. I'm still here and I'm not Captain Heroic. And Jake is still here, despite the fact he's a big, galumphing, clumsy oaf, and not even all that bright."

"Thanks," Jake said.

"My point is, if *we* could survive, are you

going to tell me Rachel and Tobias — Xena, Warrior Princess, and a Bird-boy who has to hunt his breakfast every morning — *didn't* make it? Come on, anything that wants to kill Rachel would have to be meaner than Rachel. And you know that's not even possible."

Cassie chuckled. She sniffled, too. The truth was I was talking total bull, but who knew? Maybe somehow Rachel and Tobias really did make it. It was easier to believe they did.

I've always said you make a choice in this world. You can see the world as being tragic, or you can see it as being funny. Some things just flat-out aren't funny, of course. But with very few exceptions, you can usually find the humour in life and in people. I guess if you want to see the world as being sad, terrible, unfair, boo-hoo boo-hoo, that's fine. But man, what kind of life is that?

We trudged. We stopped and dozed. We got up and trudged some more. And gradually that humongous comet in the sky grew faint as the sky began to light up with the rising sun.

Then with shocking suddenness, pop! The sun just seemed to jump up off the horizon. I tossed away my charred stump of a torch, closed my eyes, and spread my arms wide to welcome good old Mummy Sun.

It illuminated a scene out of some museum diorama. The plain stretched out before us, punctuated now with clumps of trees and sudden jutting rocks. The stream still wandered beside us. The woods were off to one side. The volcano was still smoking away, looking intimidating as it towered up above the plain.

And scattered about on that African-looking savanna, where you might expect to see gazelles or wildebeest or lions, there was a small herd of Triceratops. They moved along calmly, maybe a hundred of them. Like an old-west buffalo herd, I guess. Only Buffalo Bill would have hung up his hat rather than go after these bad boys.

<Does the rising sun make humans feel more optimistic?> Ax asked.

"Yeah. Unless it's a school day," I said.

<We are the same. It doesn't make complete sense, but it does make me feel better. I can see. Seeing is useful.>

"Plus it blanks out that comet, and that thing was starting to bug me. On the other hand, I'm looking at a bunch of dinosaurs the size of cement trucks, so—"

<The comet bothered you? But not the flash of light?>

"Lightning. So what?"

<No, no. Not lightning. I assumed you knew.

It was artificial in origin, not natural.>

It took me about five more steps before I said, "What?" I stopped. Jake stopped. Cassie stopped.

"Artificial?" Jake asked. "What do you mean, artificial? Doesn't that mean man-made? Or at least, *made*?"

<Yes, of course. The flash was not a naturally occurring phenomenon. It was all wrong for lightning. My stalk eyes are capable of seeing a little further into the ultra-violet and infra-red spectra of light and—>

"Just tell us what it was!" Cassie yelled impatiently. That shocked us all. Cassie never yells. But then again, maybe she's just not a morning person.

<I believe it was an explosion. I would have thought it was a Dracon beam striking a target, only it was too blue.>

Jake took a deep breath. "Ax? Do me a favour. Don't assume we know these things, OK?"

<Yes, Prince Jake,> he said.

Jake looked at me. "You think Yeerks got transported back to this time with us somehow?"

<Prince Jake, I don't—>

"Don't call me prince," Jake said automatically.

"There weren't any Yeerks anywhere near

that submarine when it blew up," I said. "Especially not any Yeerk spacecraft. I mean, come on, I think we'd have noticed."

<It isn't the Yeerks,> Ax said. <I assumed there must be some sort of highly advanced species of these dinosaurs. But it isn't the Yeerks.>

"Highly advanced dinosaurs?" I said. "Professor T-rex? I don't think so."

"Last night I saw some weird flashes far off," Jake said.

"Me, too," Cassie said. "I assumed they were lightning or something."

We resumed walking. "Ax-man, I think maybe you're just nuts."

<Me? Wrong? It is possible,> Ax said dubiously. <But the nature of the light certainly seemed to. . .>

He droned on for a while about the wavelengths and the retinal impact patterns and distance-sense and a lot of other Andalite stuff that humans would probably learn about someday.

I tuned it out. I was watching the Triceratops herd, which was off to our side now. I mean, come on, every little kid has a toy plastic Triceratops at some time. And here they were. Real. Actual dinosaurs moving along, munching the grass, occasionally using their huge long horns to dig up a tasty herb. It was cool. Set aside the fact that we had taken a big lift-ride about ten floors down on the food chain. It was still cool.

"Oh, man, look. I think we're coming up on some kind of big gorge or what ever," Jake said.

The prairie before us did seem to stop suddenly. The grass wasn't waving beyond a certain point.

"We'll have to go around," Cassie said.

"Why?" I wondered. "Where exactly is it we think we're going?"

"What do you want us to do?" Jake asked peevishly. "Sit down right here and start building a new civilization?"

"I'm just saying it's not like we have an appointment to be somewhere."

We marched on, unable to see the extent of the rift till we got close.

And then suddenly we could see. It was incredible. Like walking up on the Grand Canyon the first time. We were at the edge of a valley three hundred metres deep and a few kilometres across. It gave me vertigo just standing there, like I might fall in.

And it would be a very long fall, with plenty of time to scream on the way down.

But that wasn't what really knocked the wind out of us. Because see, the valley wasn't empty. Down there, spread across two kilometres of valley floor, were glittering, shining buildings.

Buildings.

And hovering protectively above those buildings was something that looked an awful lot like a flying saucer.

Chapter 20

 Tobias

"**H**ow's the wing?" Rachel asked.

<It itches. How are your feet?>

"They hurt all over again."

<Am I hurting your shoulder?>

"Nope. Not like you hurt my stomach when you opened me up like you were gutting a fish."

<I said I'm sorry. I've said it over and over.>

"I know. I'm cranky. I didn't exactly have a good night's sleep. I seem to remember having to morph the grizzly bear, only to have you come along and slice me up like I was a pepperoni pizza. Slice me up like I was a hunk of cheese."

I sighed. I tried to balance on Rachel's shoulder without digging my talons in. We'd ripped a patch of the dead Deinonychus's skin to cover her shoulder, but it wasn't staying on.

"Sliced me up like I was a ham," Rachel muttered. "Like I was bacon. And eggs. And some hash browns. Denny's. I'd give up shopping for a Denny's Grand Slam breakfast right now. The one with the pancakes. Get the hash browns as a side order. Two sausage links, two slices of bacon, two eggs over medium, you know? Not too soft and runny. I don't like them soft and runny. Maple syrup on the pancakes. Has to be maple. What kind of person puts boysenberry syrup on pancakes?"

<So I'm guessing you're hungry?>

She turned her icy blue eyes towards me. "Like a loaf of bread. That's how you sliced me up. Like a loaf of bread you get fresh from the bakery, all crusty and crispy and golden on the outside and soft and white and still-warm inside. And raspberry preserves. Has to be raspberry. I like Smuckers. A big jar of raspberry preserves with the seeds. I mean, what kind of baby has to have seedless preserves?"

I looked at her with my hawk's eyes. I was

centimetres away. It was like looking at her through a microscope, practically. She hadn't slept, hadn't brushed her hair, and she was in a bad mood. But she looked great.

I looked away. What was the point? Jeez, my own tiredness and hunger must be affecting me. I was starving. I could see little shrew-like mammals flitting between tree roots and cowering beneath ferns, but with a busted wing there was nothing I could do.

All I could do was watch the trees as we walked. We had left the Deinonychus pack behind in the night. As leader of the pack, I'd snarled at them until they backed away. I left them looking lost and stupid. But pretty soon they'd get around to choosing a new leader.

Rachel had acquired one of them. It hadn't been easy, but I'd been able to control the murderous creature long enough for her to touch him.

Now we were wandering along in the forest. Looking for food. Looking for Jake and the others. Looking for a clue of what to do.

We were entering an area with more vegetation now. There were clusters of palm trees here and there. Clumps of five or ten trees with some bushes around the base. It made me nervous. They blocked my view.

126

On the other hand. . . <Hey, don't dates grow on trees?>

"Not according to my mum. She's thinking about dating again. You know, it's been awhile since the divorce and . . . oh. You mean like dates you eat? I guess they grow on trees."

<On date palms, right?>

"Like I know? Like I go food shopping out in the wild? Picking dates off trees and tomatoes off vines and corn out of, I don't know, corn trees?"

<Corn trees? Corn trees?>

"Oh, fine. I'm starving and you're picking on me because I'm not a farm girl like Cassie."

<We could go look at those palm trees. Maybe they have dates or coconuts in them. Something for you to eat, anyway.>

"I could use a rest. And some shade."

We headed towards the second nearest clump of trees. Two monstrously big Triceratops were over in the shade of the nearest trees. Supposedly they were peaceful plant-eaters. But they were big as elephants, with metre-long horns. So no matter how peaceful they were, I didn't want to share the shade with them.

<There's definitely something up in those trees,> I said. I could see pods of some sort clustered under the fan-like fronds.

We reached the shade of the tree. Rachel set me down on the ground and threw rocks until she knocked a pod down. It was brown, about the size of a coconut. She used another rock to bash it open. Inside was a whitish pulp.

"Well? What do you think?"

<I don't know. Most likely it won't kill you.>

Rachel made a face. She held a piece of the pulp up to her nose. "Smells OK." Then she shrugged, popped some in her mouth and swallowed. "Hmm. Not bad."

<What's it taste like?> I asked. I gazed up jealously at the fruit. I was low down on the ground, not able to see much but the towering trees. But something caught my eye. Through the smooth trunks and riotous bushes, I saw something curved. It looked ridiculously like a handheld fan. Only much bigger. There were spines or spokes with brightly-patterned green and red fabric between them.

No, not fabric. Skin. But it had to be from something dead. It wasn't moving. Totally still.

<Rachel. I think there's something just on the other side of this clump of trees. See that — yaahhh!>

The fan had moved.

Rachel froze. "Please don't tell me it's another of your dinosaurs."

<When did they start being *my* dinosaurs? Let's just back away slowly.>

Rachel reached down to lift me up. "What is it?"

<I can't see enough of it to tell.>

We backed away, keeping our eyes firmly fixed on the spotted fan or sail. But as we backed away I realized Rachel's shoulder was getting tougher to hold on to.

<What are you doing?>

"I'm morphing," she said. "I'm hungry, you're hungry. Maybe we can take this guy down and have a nice big dinosaur breakfast."

<What? What?>

"I'm morphing that dannynockorus."

<Deinonychus?>

She couldn't answer. Her tongue was no longer human. Her skin was pebbly and rough. Her shoulder sloped downward and I jumped off to land in the grass.

I wasn't exactly happy with Rachel at that point. But at the same time, I wondered if maybe she was right. We had the Deinonychus morph. Why not use it?

I began to morph myself. Great, it would mean resetting my splint yet again. This was no way to heal. Then again, starving wasn't all that good for your health, either.

The breeze shifted. The skin and bone sail moved. It moved to catch the breeze. Why? I should know. There was some fact hiding just in the back of my head. What was I forgetting?

I pictured my toy dinosaurs. Tyrannosaurus rex, Brachiosaurus, Stegosaurus, Allosaurus, Spinosaurus.

Spinosaurus?

Big sail on its back. What about it? What was it like? What did it do? Was it a herbivore?

Moving!

CRASH! CRASH! Crrrrr-UNCH!

Up rose the sail as the Spinosaurus stood up. Crash went the bushes as it swivelled to look at us. Crunch went a tree trunk as it thrust its head through the trees to get a closer look at us. The head was bigger than Rachel.

She was just completing her Deinonychus morph. Would she be able to control the dinosaur's active instincts? She was more experienced at morphing than I was.

The Spinosaurus glared at us. Or at Rachel, at least.

<He's scared of us,> she said. <He's big, but he's probably just some great big prehistoric cow, right?>

<Rachel. Look at the teeth. Do those look like herbivore teeth?>

<Oh.>

The Spinosaurus rose up to its full standing height, looming up huge behind the trees. The curved sail on its back was almost two metres high. Tail to nose it was eighteen metres long. It stood on two legs — smaller and weaker legs than a Tyrannosaurus, but plenty to move with.

The Spinosaurus was silent. It just stared as two Deinonychus emerged from a girl and a bird.

<We can still take him.>

That would be Rachel, of course. I'd never say anything so stupid. <What are you, crazy? He weighs tonnes. We weigh kilogrammes.>

<There's two of us. One of him.>

<One is plenty!>

<OK. Then let's run away.>

<Now you're talking.>

We turned. We ran.

We ran right into the Spinosaurus's mate.

Chapter 21

 Rachel

What could I do? I had to attack. The Deinonychus body was surging with power and deadly energy.

Then again, the Spinosaurus was way, way too big. To give you some idea, if we'd both been dogs, the Spinosaurus would be a German shepherd and I'd be a Chihuahua.

No choice. No way around the second Spinosaurus.

<Attack!> I yelled.

I leaped. The steel spring legs lifted me off the ground and I flew through the air, deadly raking claws outward. I was aiming for the Spinosaurus's exposed belly.

SLASH! With my oversized talons. Two bright red lines in the Spinosaurus's belly!

Two little lines that looked like something the Spinosaurus might put a Band-Aid on. The Spinosaurus looked puzzled. And then it looked annoyed. It ruffled its weird sail back and opened its jaws and looked at me like I had "Oscar Mayer" printed on my back.

<OK, forget attack. We go back to plan "B". *Run!*>

And that's when I noticed the other creature step smoothly out from the bushes.

It walked on two legs. It was rough-textured, like it had really chapped skin. It was reddish in colour. It had two big eyes and a small mouth, all of the same reddish-rust hue. It stood just under three metres tall. It was carrying a weapon.

It was not a dinosaur.

The creature raised the weapon and pointed it at the wounded and angry Spinosaurus. I saw no flash. Heard no explosion. But the Spinosaurus fell over. Like a redwood falling in the forest, it fell over.

WHAMMM!

The second Spinosaurus processed this and decided to go back to sleep.

Tobias and I stared at the rough-textured creature with the gun. <What the . . . what is *that*?>

<I don't know,> Tobias said. <But I can guarantee none of my toy dinosaurs ever carried guns.>

The creature gazed curiously at us with what seemed to be eyes, although they were mere indentations in its face. From its head a pair of antennae, flexible as whips, grew and began waving towards us.

Satisfied after a few seconds of this, the antennae were retracted.

"You may not kill those creatures. There are very few left. They are ours. All creatures are ours. All things are ours. What are *you*?" it asked in a rough, raspy, buzzing voice.

It was speaking English. Now, on *Star Trek* you see aliens speak English all the time. Like that would be normal. But in real life when you encounter an alien speaking English, it's just weird. You figure at the very least they should be speaking Russian or Japanese or something.

"Answer."

<We're . . . dinosaurs,> I said, feeling fairly idiotic.

"You speak now without making sound. Explain."

<Why don't *you* explain?> I said. <Who are you? What are you doing here? And how do you speak our language?>

"We hear while you are talking. Listening long time. Since night."

<How did this guy manage to follow us and listen in?> I asked Tobias.

<I don't know. I would have seen him.>

"Change to your other form."

<He's seen us morph.>

<What *are* you?> Tobias demanded.

"We are the Nesk. This is our planet. Change to your other form."

<Pushy, isn't he?> I said.

<He's got the gun.>

<I don't like him. He smells, for one thing. And the smell . . . something familiar about it. Something wrong. I can't quite remember. Can't quite place it. But something's wrong.>

"This weapon can cause creatures to become unconscious. This happened to the great beast you were attacking. But it can also cause death. Change into your other forms. Or I will cause your death."

The Nesk raised the weapon and pointed it at us.

Now, maybe I have to back down before an eighteen-metre-long Spinosaurus. But I've faced plenty of pushy aliens with ray guns.

I knew this Nesk character with the ego problem would expect me to charge him, like a dinosaur. But I'm a human. Better yet, I'm a gymnast. So, just like on the balance beam, I spun on one leg and whipped my rigid tail into the Nesk.

<Take that!>

My tail hit hard. It slammed into the Nesk at his chest level. My tail broke him in two. The top half simply fell off. Like I'd chopped through a tree.

<Oh, my God!> I cried, horrified. I'd only intended to knock him down.

But then my horror changed tone. The severed lower body seemed to be dissolving. Breaking into thousands and tens of thousands of tiny squirming pieces!

And the fallen upper body was still holding the weapon. Raising it towards me again!

No time for pity. I lunged, mouth wide-open. I bit down on that raised hand.

It dissolved. Crumbled. I felt a squirming in my mouth. Then stinging, burning. I spat out the gun. It hit the dirt. And a wave made up of the Nesk's body parts raced to reach it.

My mouth was still alive with stinging and burning. The tiny reddish body parts began to crawl out of my jaw, up onto my muzzle. Up where my eyes could see them clearly.

Then I remembered that smell. The acrid smell of a tunnel, the stink of deadly automatons racing to tear me apart.

Ants!

The Nesk was made up of millions and millions of ants.

Chapter 22

 Cassie

"**O**K, those buildings were *not* built by dinosaurs," Marco said.

Jake looked at Ax. "Ax? Do you have any idea what is going on here?"

Ax looked as puzzled as he was capable of looking. <You are sure this is not some unknown chapter of human history?>

"Ax, at this point humans aren't even a gleam in some tiny mammal's eye. We're a long, long way from seeing the first primate. Let alone an actual human. Could they be Andalites?"

<They are not Andalites,> Ax said. <We, too, have not yet evolved by this point. In fact, I believe our planet is still wandering between two different stars, one of which will later go nova, but in such a way that the shock wave will—>

"A simple 'no' would do," Marco interrupted.

<They are certainly not Taxxons, Hork-Bajir, or even Yeerks. None of those species exists yet.>

"The Pemalites?" I suggested. We knew of the Pemalites from Erek. Erek looked and acted like a normal kid, but he was actually an android — a Chee — built by the extinct race called Pemalites.

Marco shook his head. "Erek told us when they arrived on Earth, the last Pemalites were dying. The Chee joined their essence or whatever with wolves. There aren't any wolves. We're probably tens of millions of years away from wolves, too."

"So who is hanging around on Earth in this era who can build cities and flying saucers?" Jake asked impatiently.

"Why don't I go ask them?" I said, pointing to the small city in the valley. "Or at least go check them out. My osprey morph would be perfect. There are birds in this era, so I shouldn't be too obvious."

Jake nodded. "OK. That's what we'll do. We'll all go. But this just gets weirder and weirder."

"You know, only one of us has to go," I suggested. "Why don't I do it? You guys can all stay here for now."

Jake cocked an eyebrow. "What are you talking about?"

"Well, shouldn't we take the absolute minimum risk?"

Jake shook his head and kept looking at me like he couldn't figure me out.

"Look, we've already lost Rachel and Tobias," I blurted. "I lost my best friend. I don't want to lose . . . you know. Anyone else."

Marco looked like he was right on the verge of making a wisecrack. But he stopped. Still, I guess he just couldn't totally restrain himself, so he said, "Why don't I go with Cassie? Somehow I don't think it's *me* she's worried about losing." He gave Jake a sidelong smirk.

Jake rolled his eyes. "We are not going to lose anyone, OK? It's probably safer for us all to be in the air together. Here on the ground we have Big Rex to worry about."

It made sense. But it didn't make me feel

any better. It had been just twenty-four hours since I'd last seen Rachel. I hadn't had all that much time to think about her. I'd been busy staying alive. And I guess the truth is, I almost didn't want to think about her really being gone.

But last night, in that terrible black chaos, blind, unable to tell where Jake's terrified cries were coming from, I just kept thinking, *No, it can't happen again. I can't lose Jake, too.*

Now here we were, staring down at what might be our only salvation in this dangerous world. But I was more worried than before. Maybe I trust animals more than civilization.

"OK," I said. "But I get a bad feeling about this. See, this can't be right. There can't be a city down there. It doesn't make sense. There are no cities in the age of dinosaurs. And no flying saucers, either. I know we have to check it out, but we need to be careful."

I began to focus on my osprey morph. An osprey is a type of hawk that normally lives by water and eats fish.

Grey feather patterns began to appear on my skin. I saw my bare feet become talons, my arms twist into wing shapes. It was a morph I had done many times before. But it was a morph from a different world. This was a world where true birds seemed to be small in number.

There was a nice breeze blowing. And I could guess that there would be excellent thermals — warm updraughts — welling up from the steep valley walls.

<Everyone ready?> Jake asked.

<Look!> Marco yelled.

Half a dozen small dinosaurs, each standing on two legs and no more than a metre high, goggled at us with huge yellow eyes.

<Let's fly,> Jake said.

The dinosaurs attacked at a run. A very fast run.

<I am getting so sick of this place,> Marco said as we flapped into the breeze and raced along on our talons.

I reached the edge of the cliff. I opened my wings and sprang out into the void. The tiny dinosaurs stopped at the edge and watched us go.

<This does seem to be a dangerous time in Earth's history,> Ax said. <It's a wonder humans ever evolved in such a dangerous world.>

<The dinosaurs were all gone before humans evolved,> I pointed out.

<All?> Ax asked, puzzled.

<Yeah. There were no dinosaurs by the time humans began to appear. They were all wiped out much earlier.>

<Unless you count the Flintstones,> Marco said. <"Flintstones, meet the Flintstones, they're the modern stone age family.">

I'd been right about the thermals. It felt good to be floating on a warm breeze. I know this seems crazy, but I somehow felt more at home in the osprey morph than my own human body. Humans just seemed so totally out of place in this era.

We flew towards the shining city in the valley. With osprey eyes I could see much more clearly. I saw buildings that rose in steep, smooth sweeps, like they'd grown from the bedrock. Windows were stuck in odd locations, some aiming out, others more like skylights. And there were fields planted with green and arranged in neat circles instead of rows.

<"From the town of Bedrock, they're a page right out of histo-ree,"> Marco sang.

As we got closer, I could see creatures of some sort. They looked a little like large — very large — crabs. Only with shells in a wild array of colours, deep blue, spring green, orange. And while on one side there was something very much like a large pincer, on the other side there was a pair of hands.

<Those are definitely not any species I know of,> Ax volunteered.

<They don't look friendly,> Marco said.

<Marco, how can you possibly—>

WHAM!

Something hit me! I was tumbling through the air. I fell three metres, opened my wings again and veered into a breeze. I caught air. Nothing broken. <Jake!> I cried.

<Look out, it's coming around again!> Jake yelled.

I turned my head just in time to see it fill my entire field of vision. Like some monstrous bat. Green-and-yellow leather wings seven metres across. An impossibly long, bony head.

<I can't believe something that big could sneak up on me,> I said.

<There are more,> Ax said tersely.

They were dropping from caves in the valley wall. Three, four, six of them. They opened their wide leather wings and swooped towards us.

Chapter 23

 Tobias

They swarmed towards Rachel. Millions of ants. And a group of them was already reforming around the weapon, forming a sort of hand to raise it high and aim it.

I had a very low-tech idea of how to deal with that. I leaped. I landed with both feet on the ants around the weapon. And I began to stamp.

I stamped like mad with my Deinonychus feet. They weren't great feet for stamping because they were basically built like bird feet.

But they were fast. I was stamping at a rate of several stamps per second. And whatever kind of super-alien ants these might be, they couldn't stand some man-sized dinosaur stamping on them.

The Nesk broke and ran. I roared in triumph and turned to Rachel. She was avidly licking the ants off her with her long tongue.

<What on or off the Earth was that?> I said.

<I don't even want to know,> Rachel said. <I'll tell you something about your Cretaceous Park here, though. I don't like it. It's grinding my last nerve. Not bad enough we have murderous dinosaurs everywhere. Noooo, we have to have ant-creatures from planet Zeptron!>

<Zeptron?>

<It's the first word that came to mind, all right? You want to grind my nerves, too?>

<Nope. Definitely not. But maybe we should—>

Ch-ch-ch-CHEEEEEW! Ch-ch-ch-CHEEEEEW! Ch-ch-ch-CHEEEEEW!

The ground beside me exploded, like it had been ripped by an invisible plough. I jumped. Another plough mark just behind me! I saw movement. And there, racing towards us across the plain, was a gleaming, silver craft. Maybe

146

twice the size of a Bug fighter, but shaped like an elongated pyramid, long end forward.

Ch-ch-ch-CHEEEEW! Ch-ch-ch-CHEEEEW! Ch-ch-ch-CHEEEEW!

The ship fired again and blew two more furrows in the ground.

<Run!> Rachel said.

<Run!> I agreed.

We ran. Deinonychus can run when it wants to. Very fast. Maybe thirty kilometres an hour. Too bad the silver pyramid was about a thousand times faster.

But it hesitated. I glanced back and saw it pause over the spot where we'd been. A sort of tube with a scoop on the end lowered to the ground. And I swear it vacuumed up the ants we'd scattered.

It came after us again. We dodged and the craft fired, ripping tear after tear in the ground around us.

<They're playing with us!> I yelled.

<I don't like the game,> Rachel said.

<No, I mean, like cat and mouse. They can hit us any time. They're missing on purpose. They're enjoying this.>

<Or else they're herding us,> Rachel said grimly. <They want us to keep going this way.>

Directly ahead of us was a small herd of

Triceratops. Of course, small only referred to the number of animals in the herd. Each one was the size of an elephant.

<I have to be able to see what's up ahead, up past that herd,> I said. <I'm gonna leapfrog!>

<What?>

I didn't have time to explain. We reached the Triceratops. One huge bull swung his metre-long horns towards us in challenge. I side-stepped him and leaped onto the back of an equally big but less alert female.

I leaped! Soared through the air, coiled my legs, timed it just right to slam my legs down on the Triceratops's back, bounced off her, and hurtled another three metres in the air.

From up there I could see the trap. Then I was falling.

WHUMPF!

I hit, rolled, jumped up and yelled, <You were right, it's a trap! There's a whole wall of them. A whole wall of ants! Billions! The only way out is left, but there's a sheer drop there. Can't tell how deep.>

<Great! A sheer drop or a wall of space ants! Nice choice.>

<On the count of three, we dodge left and keep going no matter what. One . . . two. . .>

<Three!> Rachel yelled.

We hauled left.

Ch-ch-ch-CHEEWWW!

Explosions of earth and rock cut across our path but I didn't care. I'd seen what was up ahead. This was better.

We raced, panting and gasping, towards what looked to us like the end of the world. A sudden gap. An emptiness.

<What is it the sky divers always say before they jump?> I asked.

<Geronimo!> Rachel yelled.

<Yeah, that's it,> I said and leaped into emptiness. Rachel was three seconds behind me.

It might have been a two metre drop. It might have been three metres. Unfortunately, it was about three hundred metres.

<Aaaaaaaahhhhhhh!> I cried.

<Aaaaaaaahhhhhhh!> Rachel agreed.

Falling, falling, spinning out of control, no time to morph. I was going to die. I would be slammed against the ground far below and die.

But even as I spun crying through the air, I swear I saw bright buildings. And then, much closer, a bird. A very familiar bird. Back in my own world I have to watch out for peregrine falcons. See, every now and then one of them will actually take a shot at a hawk.

It was like some insane joke. Like fate was trying to get a good laugh at me. Dinosaurs, aliens, and now my old nemesis, a peregrine falcon.

Then I saw the other set of wings.

The eight-metre-wide wings and bony chisel-head of a creature no human had ever seen before.

Pteranodon! I thought. *I used to play with you.*

Chapter 24

 Jake

The flying dinosaurs were above us. That was the problem. We were more manoeuvrable, but they had the altitude. And slowly but surely, by circling above us, they were forcing us down and down. Down towards the glimmering city below us.

I looked in every direction. How to get away? How to get out from under this trap?

The silver flying saucer was now only seven or eight metres below us, the highest spires of the alien city just another ten metres lower than that.

We were trapped. If we went up, the flying dinosaurs. If we went down, the city full of bright, bizarre, two-handed crabs.

<Back to the cliff wall,> I said. <The thermals will be strongest there. Maybe we can get enough lift to outrun them straight up!>

We curved back towards the cliff wall. Four of us. Cassie and Marco in osprey morph, Ax as a northern harrier, and me, a peregrine falcon.

We flapped at full speed for the cliffs. I could see colonies of the flying dinosaurs nesting there on crags in shallow caves. More were taking wing.

Stupid! I was leading everyone right back towards more of the creatures. And yet it might just work.

<Get ready everyone! Hug that cliff wall!>

I was ten seconds from slamming right into the cliff. Five. Three!

Something falling towards me! Quick turn left. Two dinosaurs, looking like miniature tyrannosaurs, were falling, kicking and scrabbling. They'd leaped off the cliff! A shower of falling rock was dislodged behind them.

They fell. The leather-winged flying dinosaurs closed in on us. In a flash of swift movement, one of the falling dinosaurs reached out with its little forepaw and snagged one of the leather wings! To my utter amazement, I saw him reach with his free claw to grab the other wing tip.

The dinosaur spread the wings as far as it could. Seven metres of leathery wing. Like a hang glider. Just enough to glide with.

The second dinosaur caught a leg on a jutting rock. It slowed the fall, but only for a second, then it tumbled away. But now there was enough time. The dinosaur with the living hang glider swept towards it.

<Rachel, get ready to grab something!> the first dinosaur yelled.

It was as if someone had stuck a thousand volt wire in my ear.

<Tobias?>

<Jake?>

WHAM! Tobias aimed for Rachel and slammed into her. Rachel was knocked into the cliff wall. Tobias was able to catch a ledge. Rachel scrabbled frantically, but kept missing her hold. She tumbled into a nest of the flying dinosaurs.

There was a furious falling, rattling, screaming, dirt-flying tussle that rolled down the cliff, but when the dust cleared, there was Rachel . . . or at least a dinosaur . . . holding tight to the legs of one big leather wing and the neck of another.

She dragged them down the side of that cliff, both of them flapping madly.

I dived after her, calling to the others.

Down, down, down. Then WHAM!

She landed. But not on the valley floor. She landed in mid-air. She was crumpled on what looked like mid-air. And the two tattered, leather wings were beside her. Also in mid-air.

<Force field!> Ax yelled.

I pulled up, just as my breast-bone scraped along what seemed like a pure, clear glass roof.

The others swooped down and landed on the force field.

<Rachel?> Cassie cried. <Is that you?!>

<Of course, it's me,> Rachel said, sounding as if the idea of her being some little dinosaur who'd just jumped off a cliff, grabbed a pair of giant leather-wing dinosaurs and landed on an alien force field was totally normal. <Who else would it be?>

We were all treated to the utterly bizarre sight of an osprey attempting to hug a dinosaur.

<I know this is kind of obvious,> Marco began, <but you're both alive!>

<Of course,> Tobias said. <You think getting eaten by a Kronosaurus was going to kill us?

Nah. Or being chased by a pack of Deinonychus?>

<What are you, Dinosaur-boy?> Marco asked.

<Now you know what I've been putting up with since yesterday,> Rachel said. <This-a-saurus and that-a-saurus. Tobias rattles them off like they were, I don't know, like any normal person would rattle off the names of major clothing designers.>

<What do you call the morphs you're in?> I asked.

<Deinonychus. And those flying reptiles there are Pteranodons,> Tobias said. <Am I the only person who ever played with dinosaurs when I was little?>

<Hey. There are buildings down there,> Rachel said. <What's going on? We were being chased by these aliens who are ants but who can join together to form bodies and carry guns. He . . . or they . . . said they were the Nesk.>

Every eye turned to Ax. He sounded a little exasperated. <I don't know. Never heard of them. We are millions of years in the past, you know. I cannot be expected to know every species in the history of the galaxy.>

<At least sixty-five million years in the past,> Tobias said. <Cretaceous Age. The last age of dinosaurs.>

Marco moaned. <Oh, man. Sixty-five million

years! I thought it was just maybe six or seven million years. I was holding out hope that we'd find some primitive people. You know, like in that old movie *Quest for Fire*? Only the babe tribe, not the hairy tribe. There would be this primitive tribe and because of my superior knowledge I would become their ruler.>

<Your superior knowledge of *what*, Marco? Your superior knowledge of Spider-Man's super powers?> Rachel asked scornfully. <You run into a tribe of Neanderthals, you'd end up being their pet monkey.>

Everyone laughed. Even Marco. It was good having the group together again. But I had to get us moving.

<Excuse me, but we seem to be standing on a force field thirty metres or so above a valley filled with aliens. Maybe we should leave. Unfortunately, there are still a bunch of mad Pteranodons above us.>

<And maybe a small ship full of those Nesk whatevers,> Tobias pointed out. <Are they the same aliens who are down in this valley?>

<No,> a voice said. <The Nesk and the Mercora are not the same.>

I looked at Ax. He looked at me. Everyone looked at everyone else. None of us had spoken. None of us even knew the word "mercora".

Out across the force field, they appeared very gradually. At first there was just a ripple in the air, then a sort of bad TV picture full of static. Then the picture was clear and real and three-dimensional.

<A localized, force-field-derived sensor shield!> Ax said enthusiastically. <Excellent!>

We were face-to-face with the aliens. Not that we could be sure where the face was, exactly.

Chapter 25

 Ax

We Andalites know more about alien races than anyone in the galaxy. We have been in space longer and travelled farther. Plus, we are scientists as well as warriors, so when we find a new race we study it. As opposed to wiping it out or enslaving it, as the Yeerks do.

We know of the Gedds and Hork-Bajir and Taxxons, the Korla, the Skrit Na, the humans, and many, many others.

But this race, these Mercora, were just

strange. For one thing, they were not at all symmetrical.

There were three of the creatures. They moved upon seven legs. Four on one side, three on the other. To make matters worse, the four legs were larger than the three. So they scuttled sideways in the direction of the small legs.

They stood about half the height of a tall human, and just less than three metres wide.

On the side with the four big legs, there was a sort of three-way pincer claw. It looked very powerful. It looked like the sort of thing I would not want to have to fight against.

On the other side, the weak side, there were two arms similar to my own, but even stronger than human arms. The arms ended in long, tapered, delicate fingers.

There were a lot of eyes. They kept opening and shutting, one or two or three at a time. They were each hidden beneath tiny trap doors in the Mercora's exoskeleton or shell. Eyes were for ever appearing and disappearing. It was very, very distracting.

<Finally,> Marco muttered. <Someone who can win a staring contest with Ax.>

<We are the Mercora,> one of them said in thought-speak. <We are immigrants to this planet. We thought we had encountered most of

the many species on this planet. But we have never encountered an intelligent species here before.>

<They think we're intelligent,> Rachel whispered. <So, Marco, keep quiet. We don't want them to learn the truth.>

It is strange the way humans will resort to what they call humour when they are frightened. Once again it struck me as strange that they had risen to dominate the very dangerous and hostile environment of Earth. I wondered how well they would have fared if they had co-existed with the dinosaurs.

<May I ask what you call yourselves?> the Mercora spokesman said.

<Is it safe to tell them the truth?> Cassie asked us all privately.

<We're sixty-five million years before the first Yeerk will show up on Earth,> Prince Jake said. <And maybe these Mercora can help us get back home.>

Prince Jake stepped forward. As well as a falcon walking on a force field could step. <We are called humans. Except for this one. . .> He tilted his head toward me. <He is an Andalite.>

The Mercora looked confused. Maybe. It was hard to tell. I can barely interpret human facial expressions. But in any case it opened and closed groups of eyes in rapid succession.

<Do you inhabit this continent?>

<Well. . .> Prince Jake said. <That's kind of a long story. Um, Ax? You probably can explain better than I can.>

<Yes, Prince Jake. We are from the future,> I said.

<Hey, that's a much better explanation than Jake could have come up with,> Marco said. <"We are from the future." Thank goodness we have a brilliant alien Space-boy here who can explain things.>

<The future?> the Mercora said. <How far in the future?>

<A . . . a long, long way,> I responded.

<Not to get all technical or anything,> Marco said drily. <Look, sir, ma'am, what ever you are, Mr or Ms Mercora, we aren't what we seem. If you promise not to tell some people who won't even exist for another sixty-five million years, we'll show you, OK?>

<Yeah, let's do it,> Prince Jake said. <What do we have to lose?>

<Aside from our lives,> Rachel added drily.

<My decision,> Prince Jake said heavily. <I think we should demorph.>

I began to do so. It must have been a bizarre sight for the Mercora. They each opened a startling number of eyes. Tobias went from dinosaur to hawk. Rachel from dinosaur to human. Cassie, Marco, and Prince Jake from bird to human. And I morphed from bird to Andalite.

<As you see,> I explained, <we are two different species. They are human. I am Andalite.>

<And what is he?> the Mercora asked, pointing both hands at Tobias.

<He is a human, but he suffered an accident and was trapped in his morph.>

<You are a strange species,> the Mercora said. <But you are welcome as long as you come in peace and do not serve the Nesk.>

"It was the Nesk that chased us here," Rachel said.

<Now it speaks with sound!> the Mercora commented.

"Yes, *it* does that when it's not in morph," Rachel said. "I get the idea you and the Nesk don't get along."

<They are attempting to destroy us. They want this planet for themselves. We do not wish to leave. This is our world now. Our original planet was destroyed when our sun was drawn towards a black hole. We are all that is left of the Mercora. And we cannot leave this planet. Not that we would ever wish to. It is wonderful. Wonderful. And it will be our home forever.>

A second Mercora spoke up. <What planet in the future are you from, you humans and Andalites?>

Cassie started to answer. "Actually, we're from Earth. Which is our name for—"

Suddenly she fell silent and looked shocked. Tobias was staring intensely at her. And then he spoke to me in the personal, private thought-speak whisper he'd used to silence Cassie. A whisper the Mercora could not hear.

<No one tell them we're from this planet,> Tobias said. <Hear me? No one tells them this is our planet.>

For a moment I was surprised. Slowly, understanding dawned on me.

The Mercora were wrong: they were not going to be a part of Earth's future. They were destined either to leave . . . or to be destroyed.

Chapter 26

 Marco

"You know, for being big, lopsided crabs with way too many eyeballs, these guys are really all right," I said, as I reclined against a force field shaped into an easy chair and tinted an attractive blue.

A day had gone by. The Mercora had speed-healed Tobias's busted wing, fed us, custom-designed a place for us to stay, and even attempted to make clothing for us. I was feeling pretty relaxed, gazing out of a window down at the Mercora who were busily working in the fields tending their broccoli.

Yes, broccoli. Turns out broccoli isn't even from Earth originally. The Mercora imported it from their home planet. Which explains a lot, I think.

"We have a nice apartment. We have food. Sadly, it's all vegetables, but hey, later we can introduce the concept of the McRex: two all-Tyrannosaurus patties, special sauce, lettuce, cheese, pickles, onions on a sesame seed bun. The McRex, the Quarter Tonner with cheese. And not to be impolite about our new pals here, but I'll bet these Mercora would be pretty tasty served with some melted butter."

"What are we *doing* here?" Rachel demanded. "What are we going to do, just sit around on these comfy force fields, eat broccoli, and listen to Marco babble like an idiot?"

That's when Ax came back in the room. He'd been talking to the Mercora. They found it easier communicating with him because he uses thought-speak like they do.

<I have questioned the Mercora,> Ax announced. <In order to repair the *Sario Rip* and snap us back to our own time, they say — and I agree — that we would need an explosion of great power. At least as great as the power of

that fusion weapon aboard the submarine. The Mercora point out that such an explosion would annihilate this entire settlement.>

"So? We do the explosion out in the country-side," Rachel said.

"And wipe out a few hundred thousand dinosaurs?" Cassie said.

"Besides," Jake pointed out, "the Mercora have already told us they don't control the countryside. Out there, beyond the force field, the Nesk are more powerful."

I reached down and snagged a carrot stick from a little ice bowl. At least carrots were from Earth. I munched it, thought about making a Bugs Bunny joke, decided the joke I had in mind wasn't all that funny, then said, "Look, we all want to get back, right? Our families. My dad. But either we can or we can't. If we can't, absolutely *can't*, then maybe we should just try and make the best of this."

Ax came over to stand by the window. He looked out with his main eyes. One stalk eye was pointed at me. The other was pointed towards the rest of the group. <The Mercora don't use explosive weapons, anyway. They would not have anything powerful enough. However. . .>

I saw Rachel's head snap around. "However *what*?"

<However, they say the Nesk do have large explosive weapons. They say the Nesk have a base thirty kilometres away. It is very well defended. No Mercora ship could hope to get close. They have a stand-off. The Nesk cannot penetrate this valley through the force field. The Mercora cannot eliminate the Nesk base.>

"Are you making a suggestion?" Jake asked Ax.

<No. Just reporting what I have learned from talking with the Mercora.>

I sat up. I looked Ax in the eye — the eye pointed towards me, that is. "OK, what are you *not* mentioning?"

Ax turned back to the group, but kept that one eyeball on me. <The Nesk are scavengers. The ships they fly, the weapons they use, are all modelled on the tools of races the Nesk have defeated. The Nesk have learned to mimic the bodies and shapes of these other races in order to fire the weapons and fly the ships. The Nesk believe the dinosaurs belong to them. As their property. They believe this planet belongs to them. But they cannot tolerate the existence of other sentient, intelligent species. They are determined to wipe out the Mercora.>

"You know, it doesn't matter if they're space ants or plain old Earth ants, ants are just not nice people," I said, and munched a second carrot.

Rachel rolled her eyes. "Ants are not nice people? There's a brilliant comment."

"OK," Jake said. "So we have two alien races fighting to control Earth. The Mercora seem basically harmless. They just want to plant broccoli—"

"That's not harmless," I muttered.

"—and live here in their valley. The Nesk, on the other hand, are aggressive and murderous. The Mercora can't help us. The Nesk maybe could help us, but won't because, after all, we're an intelligent species, too, and they don't like competition."

"Send Marco to talk to the Nesk," Rachel suggested brightly. "They won't mind him."

"Ha. Haha and also ha," I said. "Look, to get serious here, the Nesk didn't smoke that Spinosaurus that was gonna eat Rachel and Tobias, right?"

Tobias stopped preening his feathers. He was perched on the force-field table, having enjoyed a tasty prehistoric rat brought for him by the thoughtful Mercora.

<They knocked it out. It was alive, though.>

"Exactly. So I guess the Nesk don't mind dinosaurs. I mean, OK, if a Mercora flying saucer shows up at the Nesk home base, they blast it. But what if a whole different kind of army shows up there?"

Rachel suddenly grabbed my shoulder so enthusiastically it hurt. "It's a miracle! Marco actually came up with a good idea. We can morph dinosaurs and stomp on in there, set off some big honkin' explosion and maybe undo this *Sario Rip* of Ax's!"

<It is not my *Sario*—> Ax began.

"Wait a minute, why are we attacking the Nesk?" Cassie demanded. "Just because we don't like them doesn't mean we take up sides in the Mercora–Nesk war."

"Look," I said, prying Rachel's gymnast-strong fingers off my collar-bone. "We need a big explosion to hopefully close the *Sario Rip*. The Nesk have things that go 'boom'. And they aren't expecting a bunch of dinosaurs to show up asking to borrow a cup of plutonium, right? Now, that's not too complicated."

<Plutonium?> Ax snorted like I'd made a joke. <Oh, you're serious. But maybe the Nesk have slightly more advanced explosives.>

"What are you talking about?" Cassie cried. "We can't just go around picking fights like this. We all want to get back home. But we're sixty-five million years in the past. And we are not supposed to be here. Anything we do could end up changing the course of history in some terrible way."

"Ah," Jake said, nodding.

"We could do something that ends up totally altering the future without even knowing it," Cassie said. "We could . . . I don't know, we could do *something*! Something wrong."

"We could change the future so that Hanson would never have existed," I said. "I say we try!"

"You going to try and wipe out *every* guy who's cuter than you, Marco?" Rachel asked. "That's half the human race."

"Look, we can't go messing with the future," Cassie said. "It's too complicated. Too many consequences."

<Too late,> Tobias said, speaking up for the first time. <We have Homo sapiens alive here in this timeline. Not to mention me. What ever I am. See this rat I just ate? That could have been the rat that will pass on the genetic material that someday grows a smarter rat. And fifty million years from now, maybe that's the DNA, the stuff that's needed to push the earliest primate over the top. I may have wiped out the human race.> He looked down at the fur and bones. <And it wasn't even a very good rat. Too thin and stringy.>

One by one, we all looked at Jake.

"Oh, puh-leeze! I'm supposed to decide

things that may wipe out the human race?"

"You're Batman," I said. "I'm just Robin. The boy wonder," I added with a leer at Rachel.

Jake shrugged. "What are we supposed to do? Sit here and grow old, eating broccoli with the crab people? Never even try to go home?"

<There is one other consideration,> Ax said. <We are here. Which means we *were* here, sixty-five million years in Earth's past. In other words, maybe our presence here is vital to the future. Maybe we did something that *caused* the future to happen the way it happened.>

"Is anyone else's head exploding from all this?" I asked.

"Great," Jake said, stamping a few steps in frustration, then turning around again. "So if I suggest we attack the Nesk, maybe that wipes out the future. And if I suggest *not* to attack the Nesk, that could also wipe out the future. Excellent. Perfect. As long as it's all nice and clear."

<*This* decision may not be clear,> Tobias said quietly. <But another decision may be so obvious we can't ignore it.>

No one asked what he meant because at that point some Mercora showed up with more food. But I filed away his words. I filed them away in my head and I had the definite feeling I'd be double-clicking on that file again.

171

Chapter 27

 Ax

I am often amazed at Prince Jake's ability to make decisions. I call him my prince because any Andalite warrior needs a prince to serve. But I know that he is just a human youth, as I am an Andalite youth.

And yet he is very impressive for a human youth. He understands instinctively that making no decision is also a decision. So he accepts the responsibility.

If he were an Andalite I have no doubt he

would become a true prince. Still, he does very well for a human.

In the end, we decided to "go for it". That is a human expression. As I understand it, the expression means that without having any clear idea of why we should do something, we would do it anyway.

We would attack at dawn. I asked why dawn.

"Tradition," Marco said. "You do shoot-outs at high noon, you stretch in the seventh inning, you attack at dawn."

Like much of human thinking, this is a mystery to me.

"You also get executed at dawn," Cassie said.

"Thank you, Cassie, for that bit of optimism."

We had explained our plan to the Mercora. They approved. We would attack the Nesk home base and seize an explosive weapon. A bomb. A "nuke", as my human friends said. Then we would return to the ocean and attempt to explode this "nuke" in such a way that it would close the *Sario Rip* and return us to our own time.

I hoped the Mercora would have some idea how to do this. I certainly didn't. We learned about *Sario Rips* in school. But I wasn't really paying attention that day, and I can't be expected to remember all the things I learned in school. Can I?

I was sure my human friends understood this. But to be absolutely sure, I mentioned it as we sped through the night towards the Nesk base aboard a ground-hugging Mercora transport.

<Prince Jake, you do understand that I have no idea precisely how or where or when to set off an explosion that will seal the *Sario Rip*?>

"What? *What?!*"

I was mistaken. It was clear from the expression he made with his human mouth, and the way his voice became loud and rose at the end towards a sort of shriek, and also by the way his eyes alternately narrowed and expanded, that Prince Jake had not been entirely clear on this point.

<I know that we should probably create an explosion. I don't know exactly when or where. Although it should be near the point where we first emerged into this world. I am sure of that. Mostly.>

"Don't you think you might have mentioned this earlier?" Marco said. "Like *before* we signed on for this suicide mission?"

"Look, we need the nuke, right?" Rachel said. "One way or the other, we need the nuke. So let's do it."

"Oh, I hate when she says 'let's do it'," Marco moaned. "I've changed my mind now. I can learn to like broccoli."

One of the three Mercora with us scuttled around to face us. It opened half a dozen eyes in a rapid flutter. <We are close to the place we will leave you. It is on the edge of the Nesk defensive grid. As close as we can go. Approximately point zero zero zero zero two six eight light seconds from the base.>

"Which would be. . . ?" Prince Jake asked me.

<Approximately eight of your kilometres,> I translated.

"Eight kilometres? In the dark? Here in Cretaceous Park?" Marco said. "That's kind of a hike, isn't it?"

But the Mercora were firm. Any closer and the transport would be spotted and fired on. Success depended on surprise. We were to appear to be any bunch of wandering dinosaurs. Harmless to the Nesk.

The transport came to rest amid jumbled rocks. The Mercora were very advanced when it came to force fields. But their ships were clunky and slow, compared to Andalite technology. Or what would be Andalite technology in sixty-five million years.

It was very dark outside. The Mercora kept their exterior ship's lights low. And as I trotted down the ramp, the brightest thing around was the comet. It was shockingly close now. The tail would certainly brush the planet as it passed.

Dawn was still two hours away. We were to travel the eight kilometres to the Nesk base in that time and be ready to move in as soon as the sun rose on the horizon.

<Take this, Andalite,> the Mercora co-pilot said. With one of his hands he gave me a small communicator.

<A thought-speak communicator?>

<Yes. The humans could not use it, but you will be able to.>

<What is its purpose?>

<You can inform us how the mission goes,> the Mercora said.

<Are you offering to help?>

<No. We cannot risk our limited ships and equipment.>

I nodded as if I understood. But I was puzzled. The Mercora scuttled back aboard their ship. It lifted silently off the ground with an intriguing violet glow, then sped away into the darkness.

I don't know about the humans, but I felt extremely lonely. I am always alone, being the only Andalite on planet Earth. But now I was more alone than that. My own people would not exist for tens of millions of years.

We were in the dark, a very deep darkness, beneath the glowing comet, in a past that was not my own, in a past filled with destructive monsters.

From far off I heard, "Hunh-huhnroooaaarrr."

Then Prince Jake said, "OK, let's morph."

Chapter 28

 Cassie

I didn't want to be here. I didn't want to be doing this. We didn't really have a plan. We didn't truly know what we were doing. But I couldn't sit it out. No way. Not when my friends were facing danger.

I looked up. The comet was shockingly big in the sky. The tail spread a quarter of the distance from horizon to horizon. It was beautiful. But it frightened me. Ahead, in the direction of the Nesk base, there was a slight, reddish glow that seemed to hover in the air. I realized it was the summit of the volcano.

"OK, let's morph," Jake said.

There was no doubt which morph he meant. This was not a place for my osprey or my dolphin, my skunk or even my wolf. This was dinosaur country. I had only one morph that was useful in this situation.

Tyrannosaurus rex. The tyrant lizard king.

In all of Earth's history, all the millions of years and all the billions of animals that have come and gone, this one single creature was the most powerful predator.

"I can't believe I'm stuck in a lousy little Deinonychus morph," Rachel complained. "You guys all get to do Big Daddy, and Tobias and I have to be Babysaurus."

"I wish I wasn't doing it," I said.

"Yeah, right," Rachel snorted.

There are some things about Rachel I still don't understand. And things about me that must mystify her, I guess. Rachel loves the big predator morphs. I don't. I never want to hurt anyone or anything. Not even when I have to. Not even when there's no choice.

"Tell you one thing," Marco said. "If you're gonna walk around in the dark here in Cretaceous world, you want to be carrying the big guns. And

Big Rex is the biggest."

"I guess I'd rather have the Mercora's force fields," I said. "I like the way they do things: they protect themselves without having to be so violent."

<They don't seem to object to our being violent *for* them,> Tobias said.

I looked to see him in the dark. He was already morphing. A man-sized dinosaur was growing from a bird.

"Let's just do this, all right?" Marco said impatiently. "I've been on the wrong end of a fight with a Tyrannosaurus, OK? I don't want to be standing around here debating in the dark when another one shows up looking for an early breakfast."

Jake said, "Rachel, Tobias, you guys keep an eye on us. These are new morphs for the four of us. We may have some trouble adjusting."

I took a deep breath. I guess I'd been hoping somehow we'd change our minds. But the time had come.

I focused my mind on the Tyrannosaurus whose DNA was within me. And I let the changes begin.

I expected to sprout right up. But the first changes were more subtle. My skin became rough and slightly loose. Like it didn't quite fit.

Lizard skin. Crocodile skin.

My hands split in two. My thumb and next two fingers melted together. My two smaller fingers did the same. And then the bones grew out through the lizard flesh. The finger bones grew and came to a point, two small but wicked claws.

I felt my bones grow thick and massive. My pelvis bone swelled out against my flesh. I thought it would break through. But then I realized the growing had started. I was rising up, up from the ground.

My legs were thickening, growing. Muscle layered over muscle. Muscles much bigger than my own human body. Bone and muscle, bone and muscle.

My spine began to stretch, with a squeaking sound that radiated through my head. The base of my spine stretched out and out, longer and longer, one metre, two, three metres! And longer still.

My feet grew, spreading wide into three massive toes, each ending in a ripping, rending claw. I felt my weight settle on those feet, felt my claws sink into the moist soil as I grew by tonnes with each passing moment.

But for all that, it was the Tyrannosaurus's head that shocked me the most. My jaw went from being measured in centimetres to more than a metre. The bones grew dense and heavy. The muscles rippled beneath the gravel skin. My face bulged out and out and out. My eyes spread apart, blurring everything until they had reached their proper location, facing forward.

My head expanded, grew in every direction. Bigger, always bigger! I was towering above the ground now. Huge! I balanced on my powerful legs, tail out behind me, body forward, poised.

And then, at last, came my teeth. I felt the itching in my mouth as my pathetically tiny, my ridiculous human teeth grew. From half a centimetre to two, to six centimetres, to twelve, fourteen!

New teeth appeared. Twice my normal number. They sprouted from the bones of my massive jaws.

And I was complete. More than thirteen metres from head to tail: the length of a bus. Six metres tall: the height of a two-storey house. Seven tonnes of bone and muscle: the weight of five cars.

Power and speed and destruction made flesh. Power the world had never seen before and would never see again.

I had become Tyrannosaurus rex.

King of the dinosaurs.

Chapter 29

 Marco

Surrounded! I was surrounded by enemies! I could see them looming up around me. They would fight me for food. They would steal prey. They had entered my territory!

"RRRRROOOAAARRR!" I bellowed in rage.

"HeeeRRRROOOOAAAARRR!" they answered, one by one.

Four of us together in one place. Impossible! My territory. Mine!

"HeeeRRRROOOOAAAARRR!" I raged.

But the others did not run away. They roared back at me. Four huge voices cried, "Outrage!" We bellowed and roared our threats, but no one ran away.

I stamped my feet, one after the other. I swung my tail back and forth.

The others did the same. They stamped their feet at me. At each other. Tails were swishing madly, ripping bushes and small trees out of the ground. The threat display was clear. Someone should back down. The only alternative was to do battle.

"HeeeRRRROOOOAAAARRR!" we each cried, swaying as we stomped, swishing our tails, tossing our heads, opening our mouths wide to display our deadly teeth.

Then . . . a scent.

We each caught it at the same time. The bellowing stopped. I turned my head towards the smell. Darkness. But the scent was there: living flesh. Prey.

<You guys, you're losing it! Jake, Cassie, Marco, you guys are losing it!>

There was prey just a few metres away. Two smaller creatures. Only two of them, and four of us. Not enough prey. The others would try to take them.

I leaped!

The little dinosaurs turned and ran. I was after them!

<Jake! Ax! Marco, you idiot! You guys are caught up in the morph! That's us you're chasing.>

Noises in my head. Meaningless. Running now, the chase was on! But the others like me were still there. Running, too. Trying to steal my prey!

<You guys are grinding my nerves! You're hunting us.>

<Rachel, we can't outrun them! But we can out-turn them, I bet.>

<Oh, this is so not fun! I'm gonna end up being breakfast for Marco. Talk about humiliation. When I say "now!" we double back on them!>

<Yeah.>

More sounds in my head. Strange. Disturbing.

<Now!>

The two swift, small creatures suddenly stopped and ran straight for me. In a flash, they were past. I stopped. I blinked. I was confused.

But then I smelled new prey. More this time! Close by. The wind was in my face. I knew this was a good thing. When the wind was in my face, the prey did not flee as quickly.

I quickly forgot the two small creatures and advanced towards the herd I smelled up ahead in the darkness.

<I have never seen a morph take over this totally.>

<I know. I'm starting to worry.>

<Jake! It's me, Rachel. Snap out of it. Cassie, buddy. It's me, Rachel. You're being controlled by the morph.>

The prey was close now. Yes, I could smell them. I glanced at the others like myself. Marching beside me through the darkness. Many prey this time. Enough for all.

Closer . . . closer. . .

Attack!

I bounded forward at full speed. Attack! Tail out behind me, head held forward, I raced towards the helpless prey!

In the darkness I saw a shape. Prey! I saw the bulk, the curved back. I saw the horns. Two very long and a shorter one.

The horns disturbed me. But too late to do anything but attack! Nothing could stop me. Nothing could escape.

The horns turned towards me.

Hmmm.

I dodged left. The horns turned.

Hmmm.

I slowed down. I stopped.

"Shnorf! Shnorf!" the horned creature said.

I saw the others like myself. All were staring

186

at the horned creatures. All had stopped their attack.

<Maybe now they're calmer,> the voice in my head said. <Um, you guys? Those are Triceratops.>

Huh?

<Jake, Ax, Cassie, Marco, get a grip. You are in morph.>

In morph? Me? Marco?

Yaaahhh! My brain snapped back suddenly. Instantly I was me again. OK, me again in a body that was seven thousand kilogrammes' worth of trouble.

But at that exact moment, one of us attacked.

"ROOOOAAAARRR!" A Tyrannosaurus leaped suddenly to the right, jerked its head left, and chomped its humongous jaws down on the arched spine of a Triceratops.

"Rrr-EEEEE, Rrr-EEEEE!" the Triceratops screamed. And then everything went completely insane. The Triceratops staring up at me lunged. Deadly metre-long horns were aimed at my belly, propelled by six tonnes of weight.

I jumped back, centimetres from being gored.

Another Big Rex — I don't know if it was Jake or Cassie or Ax — went roaring into battle. The massive jaw tried to clamp on one horn and hold it.

The battle was on. Tyrannosaurus versus Triceratops. The battle every kid with toy dinosaurs imagines. It was sheer, screaming madness.

<You idiots!> Rachel roared. <Back away! Back away!>

But then she and Tobias joined the fray, trying to help. They were tiny, but they could attack the lumbering elephant-sized Triceratops with more agility than we could.

My own opponent shnorf-shnorfed a couple of times, then came after me again. I backed away. I didn't need this fight.

<Aaaahhh!> I tripped, staggered back on one knee, and began to fall over. I reached to use my hands, but they were useless. I hit the dirt on my side.

The Triceratops was on me!

<Aaarrrgghhh!> A metre of horn rammed into me. It caught between two ribs. The pain was shocking and immediate.

But now the Triceratops was vulnerable. Its dangerous horns were stuck, and its front leg was in reach. I opened my jaw, jerked my huge head forward, and clamped down with all my might.

The Triceratops backed away. I released his leg and snapped at his side and missed. He lunged again. I was still down, still on my side, bleeding. I swung my legs forward and shoved my taloned feet in his face. I caught the closest horn between my toes and shoved back with all my might.

I went scooting backwards under the impact of the Triceratops's charge, but those horns didn't get me. Not this time.

I rolled into something that splintered and crashed. A tree! I had just knocked over a tree. I scrambled up, not an easy thing to do when you're a Tyrannosaurus. I got to my feet just as the Triceratops charged again. I backed away, but now there were trees all around me, hemming me in like a cage.

Then, in the darkness, the shocking sight of another Big Rex. It leaped on my Triceratops! It opened its mouth wide, and then sank three dozen or more fifteen-centimetre-long teeth into the Triceratops's neck.

"HoooRRROOOOAAARRR!"

"Rrrr-EEEEEEE! Rrrr-EEEEEEE!"

In fury and rage, the big predator yanked the front of the Triceratops up off the ground. An animal the size of an elephant, simply yanked up off the ground.

The Tyrannosaurus shook its head, shaking the screaming Triceratops like a dog worrying a bone.

And then, the Triceratops stopped making sounds. It hung limp. The Tyrannosaurus dropped it and stood over the fallen creature.

"Huh-huh-huh-RRRRRROOOOOAAAARRR!" it bellowed in triumph. The sound shook the leaves in the trees. It rattled through my wounded belly.

"Huh-huh-huh-RRRRRROOOOOAAAARRR!" it screamed again.

It was all the violence of nature, all the ruthlessness of the survival of the fittest, all the power of muscle and bone and claw and tooth, all the ageless, never-ending lust for conquest wrapped into one awesome roar.

I braced myself, afraid it might attack me next.

<Jake? Is that you?> I asked.

<No,> a thought-speak voice replied.

Chapter 30

 Jake

Cassie stood roaring over the fallen Triceratops. She was the only one still caught up in the Tyrannosaurus's mind. It scared me. It scared me for her. She hadn't wanted to do this morph. And now it had seized control of her. Gentle Cassie was trapped in the mind of a killer.

She swung her head round and glared at me, eyes mad with rage.

<What do we do?> Rachel demanded.

She was scared, too. It scared me all over

again, knowing that Rachel was scared. Rachel doesn't scare easily.

<Cassie!> Marco yelled. <Snap out of it!>

Cassie hunched over the Triceratops and began chowing down. It was an unbelievably gross scene. The sun was just coming up, and there in the pink glow, a creature as tall as a tree was devouring a creature the size of an elephant.

I took a step forward on my massive clawed feet.

Cassie spun her head round and bellowed a threat: <Stay away. It's *mine*!>

<Jake, you have to stay back,> Tobias said. <You are invading her territory. That's her prey. She'll have no choice but to defend it. She'll annihilate you.>

<No. She might annihilate this Tyrannosaurus morph,> I said. <But she would never hurt *me*.>

I knew what I had to do. I began to demorph.

<Prince Jake! That is foolish! You will look like another prey animal to her!>

<No. She won't hurt me. She'll recognize me.> I was shrinking already.

<Jake, look,> Marco said, <you may be exaggerating your charm, you know? And if she goes for you, that means we have to try and stop her.>

I hesitated. Marco was right. What if Cassie attacked? But I continued demorphing, shrinking, growing smaller and weaker all the time. The three tyrannosaurs loomed larger and larger above me. They looked to me like Tobias must look to a mouse. Even the Triceratops seemed as vast as a beached whale.

Cassie watched me, curious. Her forward-looking yellow eyes glanced at me, then at her kill, then belligerently at the other dinosaurs.

And then, slowly, slowly, as my own flesh emerged, as my hands grew human fingers, as my face flattened and hair grew and toes replaced claws, she blinked.

<Oh, my God. What have I done?> she asked. She backed away from the Triceratops.

"It's OK, Cassie," I said. "It was just a dinosaur." It was all I could think of to say. I knew it wouldn't help. You can't say "just" an animal to Cassie.

<You got caught up in the morph,> Rachel said. <It happens. All four of you did it.>

<Oh my God!> Cassie cried in horror.

<Cassie, look, it's not your fault,> Rachel said. <It was the Tyrannosaurus. It was just being itself, you know?>

<I told you guys I didn't want to do this morph!> Cassie yelled. She began demorphing.

But at the same time, I was returning to the Tyrannosaurus morph.

"Cassie, you have to stay in morph," I said. "We have a mission."

<No! I don't have to be this . . . this . . . killer!>

<Yes, you do, because we need to go kick some butt on these space ants, all right?> Marco said.

<Cassie, come on,> Rachel said. <We need you.>

<I destroyed a living creature. A fantastic living creature,> Cassie mourned.

<Cassie, get over it. This is the late Cretaceous, according to Bird-boy here,> Marco said coldly. <There are no humans. No human civilization. No human morality or religion or philosophy. This is hardcore nature. We're down to survival, here. *Survival*. That's all that counts.>

<Surviving and getting home,> Rachel amended.

<There *are* humans here,> Cassie said. <Us. We *are* human civilization. We have all that stuff inside us. It doesn't matter what year it is.>

<OK, you're right,> Marco snapped. <It doesn't matter. If this were 1998 or 2000 or 2121, it would still come down to surviving. And when it's down to kill or be killed, all that

morality and guilt and all is crap.>

Cassie stopped morphing. For a while no one said anything. Then, at last, Cassie said, <You know something, Marco? You're my friend. I'd do almost anything for you. But you're wrong. Yeah, we're just animals ourselves. But we're the animals who can think. We're the animals who can imagine something better than kill or be killed. I don't think predators are immoral. I'm not an idiot, whatever you may think. But I'm a human, OK? And I have to think and care, and I have to feel things. Otherwise I might as well be some gangster, or a Nazi or, or—>

<A Yeerk,> Ax supplied.

I had finished morphing back to Tyrannosaurus. I waited for Marco to toss out some clever come-back. It never came. Instead, as we once again headed for the Nesk camp, I heard him whisper so that no one but me could hear:

<You know, Jake? I see why you like that girl.>

Chapter 31

Ax

The sun had fully risen by the time we arrived at the Nesk base. It was near the lowest slopes of the volcano at a place where a rushing stream came down through the pock-marked grey rocks and gave rise to sparse vegetation.

It was very obviously a military base, not like the peaceful agricultural town the Mercora had built. There were perimeter defences in the form of robot towers ten metres tall. The towers bristled with several different types of energy weapons. I could see that widely differing technologies were in use. Obviously the Mercora were correct: the Nesk were scavengers. They had stolen these weapons from a variety of races.

The same was true of the spacecraft parked within the camp. There were two of the small pyramidal ships Rachel and Tobias had described. But there was also a ship in the more classic aerofoil design, as well as very odd oval-shaped craft.

There was little obvious activity within the camp. But then, the Nesk are a strange race. Essentially social insects with the ability to unite and co-operate to a stunning degree. The "bodies" they formed were only assembled in order to operate the weapons and ships they had stolen. The rest of the time, I assumed, they remained as insects.

<OK, everybody keep moving forward. Casual. Like we're all out for a nice morning walk. Ax, what do you make of it?> Prince Jake asked.

<I think the Mercora were correct and the Nesk have no interest in dinosaurs,> I said. <Those two creatures over there may have walked right through the base, judging by their present location.>

<Iguanodons,> Tobias said.

<Do you see the mound?> Cassie asked. <Looks like a dirt pile, except it's so tall and narrow? That may be their mound. Like a termite mound. That's where their queen will be.>

I had seen the mound. But I hadn't paid it any attention. Now I looked closer. <The mound is defended. Motion detectors tied to what are probably stun weapons. Dinosaurs may travel freely through the base, but the Nesk protect their mound.>

<So where do we find these alleged nukes?> Rachel asked impatiently.

<Warehouses or storage rooms over there,> Marco said. <Three of them in a row. If it were me, I'd put my most valuable stuff in the middle one. It's more protected. On the other hand, I don't see any guards.>

<I agree,> I said. <But there are probably thousands of guards. Remember, the Nesk will only assemble into a larger creature if they have to hold weapons. But the individual insects are everywhere throughout the camp.>

<OK,> Prince Jake said. <Here's what we do. Ax and Rachel, head straight for the centre warehouse. Ax to point out a nuke, Rachel to grab it, because those Deinonychus hands work better than the Big Rex's. Marco and Tobias flank to the left. Me and Cassie to the right. We

rip open that store-room, get what we came for, and head for the trees over there.>

I felt nervous. Not about possible battle. Well, yes, about that, too. But mostly, I felt nervous about identifying the "nuke". Explosive weapons come in thousands of different shapes and sizes. Some are as big as human automobiles, most are much smaller. Andalite explosive weapons are usually no bigger than a human baseball.

<Ready?> Prince Jake asked.

<Been ready,> Rachel grumbled.

<OK, everyone just keep moving like we're dinosaurs.>

<Which, thanks to the fact that our lives are totally, completely INSANE, we actually *are*,> Marco said. <I mean, does anyone else think it's just plain weird that we're dinosaurs, getting ready to steal a nuclear weapon from a bunch of ant-like aliens, sixty-five million years before the first human being ever said, "Hey, I know what, let's try *cooking* the meat this time?" Does anyone else find this slightly nuts?>

<Nope,> Rachel said.

We advanced on the base, not exactly stealthily. There was a definite impact sound each time my Tyrannosaurus foot hit the ground.

I focused on the centre store-room. I glanced

over to the trees. The Nesk ships would have a hard time following us through the trees. But getting to them would be difficult. Especially if it took me a while to find what we were after.

The base seemed empty, deserted. But when I focused my Tyrannosaurus eyes, I could see narrow columns of the ant-like creatures spreading out like a web across the entire area. When I lowered my foot near one of the columns, it simply swerved aside.

We passed closer to the small, oval ship. It was perhaps twice the size of an Andalite fighter, but it was made up of three interlocking oval tubes. I wished I had time to study it.

The store-room, just ahead. It had appeared to be built of crude metal. But when I got closer, I could see that it was actually dirt. It had been built in just the same way as the mound, by the labour of millions of the tiny creatures. Then, it had been covered in some sort of residue and polished till it was bright.

<A bizarre race, these Nesk,> I said. <They have stolen and made use of amazingly sophisticated technology. Yet at the same time—>

Scrr-EEEEEE-eeeee-EEEEEE-eeee-eeee. Scrr-EEEEEE-eeeee-EEEEE-eeee-eeee!

A screaming siren! Flashing lights! The robot defence towers blazed with green and blue light.

The spacecraft began to power up.

The entire base was suddenly very alive. Very, dangerously, alive!

<A thought-speak detector!> I cried. <They know the Mercora use thought-speak and they have a thought-speak detector!>

<What, are you kidding?> Marco demanded. <How is that possible?>

<Actually, our own Andalite scientists have been trying for years to develop such a system. It would work on the principle of—>

Scrr-EEEEEE-eeeee-EEEEEE-eeee-eeee. Scrr-EEEEE-eeeee-EEEEE-eeee-eeee!

<Here they come!> Cassie yelled. <From the mound! Here they come!>

A red-black river of Nesk poured from the mound. More belched up from the ground beneath us. The soil was alive with them! Millions, millions of them.

<Let's do this!> Rachel cried.

I leaped toward the warehouse. I kicked with my powerful Tyrannosaurus leg and knocked a small hole in the walls. I kicked again. The hole grew only slightly.

<Marco! Go help Ax!> Prince Jake said.

Soon there were two tyrannosaurs attacking the mud wall.

<This is so Godzilla!> Marco said with a

giddy laugh. <After this, we head for Tokyo!>

Suddenly, the wall collapsed. I was inside. But I was too tall! My head emerged above the roof of the building. I would have to crumble the roof, too. And each chunk of roof that fell hid more of the things inside the store-room.

Rachel vaulted past me and began to dig through boxes and crates, the stolen remnants of a dozen alien civilizations. She used her claws to rip them open, scattering their contents, even as chunks of the roof fell on her.

<The ships are starting to get off the ground!> Tobias yelled.

<Prince Jake,> I said urgently. <You can attack the ships more easily *before* they get in the air!>

<Yeah, I thought of that,> he said grimly. <Ax, you and Rachel stay on it, man. Everyone else, let's see just how much damage these dinos can do.>

Chapter 32

 Tobias

One minute we were standing in a ghost town. The next minute it was like being trapped in the middle of an out-of-control video arcade. Lights! Sirens! Spaceships powering up. The robot security towers shining broad-spectrum flood-lights everywhere.

And worst of all, millions of Nesk every-where! But they hadn't attacked us.

<They haven't figured out it's us,> I said. <They don't know where the thought-speak is

coming from. They haven't figured out it's coming from us.>

<They will, soon enough,> Rachel said. <Ax and I are ripping their building apart. They'll figure it out.>

<That weird oval-looking ship is powering up fastest,> Jake said. <Let's get it.>

Three huge tyrannosaurs began stamping towards the ship. I ran ahead of them, faster and more agile in my Deinonychus morph. There wasn't much I could do to damage the ship. Except. . .

I leaped, landed on the outer oval, just as the ship began to rise from the ground.

Crunch!

My weight tipped the ship sideways, slamming the outer ring down into the dirt. And then. . .

WHAMMM!

It was like having someone drop a house on the other end of your seesaw.

I flew through the air, cartwheeled, landed on my dinosaur butt and rolled to my feet.

Cassie had mimicked me. Only when she leaped, she leaped in a much, much larger way. Her massive tonnage ripped open the steel hull, crumpled it like aluminium foil, and flattened a segment of it in the dirt.

<Cool,> she said. <See? I don't mind stamping machines. Are you OK, Tobias?>

<Well, my dignity is hurt,> I said. <That pyramid-looking ship over there!>

We turned and raced towards the second ship.

<Found one!> Ax yelled suddenly. <I don't know the yield, but it's definitely an explosive device!>

<Then get out!> Jake cried. <Rachel, can you carry it?>

<Already have it!>

<Do we take out the pyramid ship or run?> Cassie asked.

<Ax and Rachel, get that nuke outta here, the rest of us will stay and do some more damage. Maybe make it harder for them to come after us.>

I ran for the pyramid-shaped fighter. But the Nesk had figured out what was happening. They'd made the mental breakthrough: it was the dinosaurs who'd become their enemy.

Once they figured that out, the Nesk got nasty.

TSAAAAPPPPPPPP!

A bolt of energy from the nearest robot tower blew a hole in the ground, right where I'd been standing a split second earlier. I felt a jolt of pain. The back half of my left foot was burned off!

I staggered on, but now the pyramid fighter was turning towards us, bringing its weapons to bear.

I ran full at it, but the wound slowed me down. Jake passed me and bounded through the air, tonnes of muscle and bone becoming one big projectile. He hit the pyramid fighter just as the fighter fired.

CH-CH-CH—!

WHUMPF!

The fighter went rocketing sideways, out of control. And at that moment a second robot tower fired.

TSAAAPPPPPP!

KUH-BLOOOOOOOM!

The energy weapon hit the fighter. It exploded, becoming a small sun of brilliant orange and yellow light.

The impact hit me in the side. I was in the dirt before I knew what had happened. Up I jumped, but my leg was weak as the first injury drained its strength away.

Stinging! The Nesk were all over me, biting, stinging, attacking in the most primitive way.

It was really bizarre. The Nesk were frying everything in sight with highly advanced energy weapons, and at the same time, biting.

<OK, that's it! Head for the trees!> Jake yelled.

He didn't have to tell me twice. I saw the tree line, illuminated by early dawn light and the brilliant explosions, and I moved out. Pain or no pain, I was running for cover.

But then, my injured leg just stopped working. I was down! Two gigantic tyrannosaurs lumbered by overhead. I should cry out, tell them. But if I did, they'd die trying to save me.

Like some foul-breathed saviour, there came a massive, square head. Down it came, jaws open. The jaws closed gently around me. Fifteen-centimetre teeth cut into my skin, but did not penetrate muscle.

The Tyrannosaurus lifted me up and up and up. It jolted away. Each step shot pain through my body. But at least I was up off the ground, away from the Nesk.

<Let me know if I bite too hard,> Cassie said.

CH-CH-CH-CHEEEEW!

The ground beside me erupted. Cassie was carrying me so that I was looking back. I saw the second pyramid fighter rise up and open fire. Behind it came the other undamaged fighter.

I twisted my head forward. A long, long way

to the trees. And between us and the trees, one of the deadly robot towers.

Cassie ran.

The fighters came after us.

No way. No way to make it.

<I'm going to contact the Mercora,> Ax said.

I barely had time to think *what?* when the tower opened fire. The others were all past the tower. But Cassie and I were trapped between the deadly fire from the tower and the advancing fighters.

<This doesn't look good,> I said.

<No. It doesn't.>

Suddenly, Jake and Marco turned back. They came running at the tower from behind. The tower was more than ten metres tall. The two tyrannosaurs slammed into a corner of its support beams.

CRRR-UNCH!

The tower did not fall. But it did shake. And it sagged to one side. Just enough that their next shot went wild.

Jake and Marco slammed it again, and now Cassie and I were caught up with them. Cassie gave the supports a devastating kick.

Slowly, slowly, then faster and faster, the robot tower began to fall.

It fell like a redwood, straight down towards

the Nesk mound.

It helped, but not enough. We'd been too slow. As we raced for the woods, the fighters closed in. There was no way to outrun them. No way to outmanoeuvre them. They had us cold.

We were all going to die, sixty-five million years before any of us would be born.

Chapter 33

 Rachel

We hit the tree line, me and Ax. In my front claws I held a small, oblong white tube. According to Ax, a nuclear explosive.

Let me just say this. Carrying around a nuclear weapon? That'll make you nervous.

I looked back. And I saw what was about to happen.

Three very big Rexes — Jake, Marco, and Cassie — were running. Head forward, tail back, running like roadrunners. A Deinonychus was in the mouth of one Tyrannosaurus. And two spacecraft were practically above them.

It would be point-blank slaughter now.

<The situation is hopeless,> Ax said.

<What do you mean, *hopeless?*> I demanded.

<I am speaking with the Mercora,> he explained.

I remembered him saying something earlier about that. But it was irrelevant to me.

<I'm going back for them,> I said.

<Don't be foolish, Rachel. All you would do is give the Nesk another target.>

<Exactly,> I agreed grimly. <Maybe if they're shooting at me, one of the others will get away.>

I started back out into the open. I heard Ax come lumbering behind me.

CH-CH-CH-CHEEEEW!

The pyramid ship fired.

<Aaaaahhhhhh!> Jake cried.

He fell forward, half a dinosaur.

<DEMORPH!> I screamed.

The pyramid ship turned at a leisurely pace, hovering directly above the writhing, thrashing, helpless monster who was Jake.

CH-CH-CH-CHEEEW!

At point-blank range, the Nesk pyramid ship fired.

<Nooooo!> Cassie screamed.

211

The blast was blinding. But when the flash cleared, Jake was still there! An electric glow illuminated a sort of invisible shell around him.

<Force field!> Ax said. <The Mercora!>

Then we saw the two Mercora ships. Exactly like flying saucers. One was just above the pyramid ship. It had projected the force field to protect Jake.

The Nesk pyramid fighter saw it now, too. It fired. At the same instant, the Mercora fired.

BOO-BOOOOM!

The twin explosions were almost simultaneous. The pyramid ship and the Mercora saucer both blew apart.

The remaining Mercora saucer hovered above Jake and the others. The remaining Nesk ship seemed to hesitate. And while it did, Jake and the others began to demorph.

<They're going to try and take us all aboard,> Ax said. <We should demorph. They don't have room for these bodies.>

I began to demorph, but it was an agonizing wait while the Nesk considered whether to attack or retreat.

The saucer hovered. The Nesk hovered. Stand-off.

Jake, Cassie, Marco, and Tobias all demorphed. Ax and I stepped out from the trees, out in plain view. The Nesk were looking at humans for only the second time, and they were seeing an Andalite for the first time ever.

"What do you think they're going to make of you?" I asked Ax.

<Perhaps they will think that the Mercora have acquired powerful new allies,> Ax said.

As if the Nesk had heard him, their ship suddenly veered off and retreated to the wreckage of the base.

I laughed. "Guess you're right, Ax. Looks like the Nesk have had enough. Modern age or Cretaceous, no one can beat the team of human and Andalite."

The Mercora saucer picked us up, us and our little nuke. But they were a grim, depressed bunch of aliens. It was hard to tell at first. But then I noticed that each of them was minus one of their smaller legs. There were just oozing stumps.

"What happened to your legs?" I asked. But even as the words were out of my mouth, I saw the limbs in the corner. They were laid out on a brightly coloured cloth which was draped over a shelf. There was something ceremonial about it. Almost religious.

<Can you explain the meaning of this?> Ax asked politely.

<We must make the sacrifice of pain. The legs will regenerate, but those we honour will not,> the Mercora pilot said. <This is a symbol. It speaks to our spirit's pain, by echoing it in physical pain.>

"They did this for the Mercora who were in the other ship?" Jake asked.

<For those who were in *both* ships,> the pilot said. <To be killed is a sadness. To kill is a sin.>

"You'd fit right in with these guys, Cassie," Marco said.

Cassie ignored him. "Our legs and arms do not regenerate," she said to the Mercora.

The pilot responded, <Then you must bear the pain inside.>

"Yes," Cassie said. "I will."

"Thanks for saving us. We're sorry about the Mercora on that other ship," Jake said. "We owe you. We owe you big."

"That goes for all of us," I added. "Anything we can ever do for you . . . I mean, until we get back to our own time. *Any*thing."

<Don't make promises you can't keep, Rachel,> Tobias said in a thought-speak whisper only I could hear. <It will only make it worse later.>

I looked at him for an explanation. But the eyes of a hawk give nothing away.

Chapter 34

 Tobias

Flying beneath the force field was a strange experience. Plenty of heat radiated up from the Mercora town and the fields around it, so there were stunning thermals. But the force field created a sort of glass ceiling above me that I could not hit without risking another busted wing.

A weird experience. But it was good to be flying again. And I felt like I had a sort of mission. I felt someone should see this Mercora settlement. Someone should see all that would be lost, and remember.

It was amazing, really. The universe had so many secrets. Who would have guessed that so long before the humans and the Andalites and Yeerks would even appear on the screen to play out their own life-and-death struggle, there had been an earlier war for Earth?

Through the slight distortion of the force field I could see the Pteranodons in their cliff-side nests. I wondered how they hunted and what they caught in this strange situation. But who could tell? Like all living things, they were doing their best to adapt. They were looking to eat without being eaten. Same as my life as a hawk. The same old cycle: life trying to stay alive by any means it could find. Life trying to survive the enemies of disease, hunger, fire, flood, and all the animals who were bigger and badder.

I felt the warm wind fill my wings. I turned and circled upwards till I could see the entire valley and feel the force field just centimetres above me. Somehow the Mercora had figured out how to let the rising air pass through the field. They were a smart, advanced, and decent race. I hoped somewhere out in the galaxy there were other Mercora colonies.

Down below, down on what could almost be a street, I saw my friends talking to some excited Mercora. I spilled air and began to dive. Sometimes there's nothing more relaxing than a hurtling dive through the air.

I perched on a land vehicle that was parked near the others.

<What's up?> I asked.

"The Nesk are leaving!" Cassie cried happily. "The Mercora say the Nesk have left Earth! Their orbital ships came down and removed everything from the base."

"Looks like the good guys won," Rachel said. "I think the Nesk saw that the Mercora had some new friends, some serious, butt-kicking new friends." She laughed, mocking her own bravado.

<Yeah. Guess so, huh?> I said.

The Mercora celebrated their victory that afternoon and into the evening. They celebrated by ploughing up another hundred acres at the edge of the colony and planting seeds.

The others and I went to the rooms they'd set aside for us. We ate the food they'd provided, and rested on the shaped force fields that passed for furniture.

Night fell, and through the window the comet seemed to fill the sky. I perched where I could watch it.

"So OK, now we have to figure out where and when to use this nuke," Jake said.

<The Mercora have agreed to let us use their computers,> Ax said. <With their help, I can probably recreate the theory behind *Sario Rips*, and then come up with an accurate plan.>

Jake nodded. "Good. Great. Take your time, Ax. Do it right."

"Yeah, why rush? We have all the broccoli we could possibly need," Marco said, making a face of utter disgust.

I watched the night deepen. I watched the head of the comet. And then, I saw it: a stab of flame that shot from the side of the bright white comet head. Blue flame, at a right angle to the trajectory of the comet.

I felt my heart skip a beat.

The Mercora noticed it, too. From the streets outside there came a wailing siren.

"What's that?" Marco asked. "Sounds like the cops."

Jake shrugged. "Who knows with the Mercora? They're some strange aliens. Maybe it's Mercora music."

Several minutes later, two Mercora came bursting into the room. Their eyes were fluttering open and shut at an alarming rate. Their two weak-looking hands were waving wildly.

<The Nesk! They cannot accept their defeat. They have decided if they cannot have this planet, then neither can we.>

"What do you mean?" Cassie asked.

<They have diverted the comet. The comet is now on a trajectory for impact on this planet. Here, on this very settlement. In little more than a day, the comet will strike.>

"We can't let that happen!" Cassie said. "You can't just give up. Isn't there some way you can . . . I don't know, push it the other way?"

The Mercora responded, <Even our most powerful force field could not move the comet. There is only one chance. The explosive device you took from the Nesk. . . We could use our last ship, carry it to the comet and explode the device. It might fragment the comet's head. However. . .>

"They don't want to ask us for the nuke," Jake said.

"That's carrying politeness a long way," Marco said. "If it was me, I'd be like, 'Hand that over, pal'."

"If we give up the nuke, we have no way home," Rachel pointed out.

"We have no choice!" Cassie said. "Are the six of us more important than this entire settlement? Are we supposed to condemn them to death just because we want to get home again?"

"Wait a minute, are you *serious*?" Marco demanded. "We're gonna give up our only ticket out of here? I don't think so."

"Ax, if that comet hits, how much damage will it do?" Jake asked.

But Ax couldn't answer. He was distracted by what I was telling him in private thought-speak. Distracted by what I was asking him to do.

To the Mercora I said, <Please give us a couple of minutes to consider. Come back then.>

They left. I met Ax's gaze. He was looking at me with his two main eyes. His stalk eyes were staring down at the small but devastating weapon he now held in his hands.

Chapter 35

 Cassie

The Mercora went away. And when they came back, we gave them the nuke.

I was surprised by the final vote. It was four to two, with Rachel and Marco against. I guess Jake felt he owed his life to the Mercora. Same as I felt. But I was surprised by the quiet way that Tobias and Ax went along. Neither of them said anything. Just voted with Jake and me.

The Mercora took the weapon and raced to

their remaining saucer. I watched from the window as it began to power up.

<We need to get out of here,> Tobias said, speaking at last.

"Why?"

<We have to be far, far from here when that comet hits.>

"What do you mean, when it hits?" I demanded. "The Mercora think this will work. They think they can break it up into small chunks that will burn up entering the atmosphere."

Tobias stared at me with his cold hawk eyes. <The nuke won't explode. Ax fixed it so it'll be a dud. And he fixed it so the Mercora won't know till it's too late.>

I just stared. We all did.

"Wait a minute," Marco said. "If we're not using it, we better hope the Mercora can! Hey, genius, we're down here, too! That comet hits and we get pounded ten kilometres down through solid rock. That's gonna hurt."

<No time to explain now,> Tobias said. <Everyone morph to birds. We need to haul out of here in a couple of minutes.>

"Tobias, what have you done?" I demanded.

<I did what had to be done, all right?!> Tobias yelled in a blaze of sudden anger. <I did

what had to be done. I made the call, so that none of you would have to feel bad about it.>

"You need to explain this right now," Jake said in the low, silky voice he uses when he's really mad.

<Start morphing or I'll explain nothing,> Tobias said. <Just do it!>

Rachel started morphing to her eagle morph. Jake hesitated, but there was a force to Tobias I'd never heard before. Jake began to morph. Then Marco. Ax. What could I do? I had to go along. I had to morph.

<It's the Cretaceous Age,> Tobias explained. <Late Cretaceous, the last age of dinosaurs.>

"So?" I demanded while I still had a human mouth.

<So what do you think happened to them all, Cassie? Dinosaurs ruled the earth for a hundred and forty million years. You've all seen how weak and helpless we are in this age. You've seen how the only mammals are tiny rats, small enough to avoid attracting the attention of the big dinosaurs. So how do you think the dinosaurs fell and the mammals rose?>

<They . . . they evolved,> I said.

<Yeah, they evolved. But evolution got a great big helping hand. See, about sixty-five million years ago . . . around now . . . something

— they don't know if it was an asteroid or a comet, but *something* — hit Earth. Very hard. Hard enough to fill the atmosphere with dust, block the sun, and bring on a colder climate. And that's how the dinosaurs died.>

<You don't know it's *this* comet!> I cried. <You don't *know*!>

<Yes, I do,> he said. <No one in our time ever found a Mercora fossil. Which means they never prospered, never populated the planet, never grew beyond this one handful, this one settlement. *This* is the comet. *This* is the time. Today is the end of the Mercora. And today . . . today is the end of the dinosaurs.>

I wanted to tell him he was wrong. But I knew he wasn't. I wanted to cry. But I had become an osprey. Birds don't cry. It was monstrous, horrible.

Inevitable.

<We're going to let these people, these Mercora, we're going to let them die?> I asked.

<I'm surprised you, of all people, don't understand, Cassie,> Tobias said. <It's about more than these Mercora. The entire planet will be changed today. A million species will begin to die. A few weeks or months or maybe years from now, the last Tyrannosaurus is going to die. And because of that, other creatures will begin

to evolve. Including. . .>

<Us,> I said. <Homo sapiens. Homo sapiens, who could never have evolved unless the dinosaurs had died out.>

<So that comet *has* to hit,> Rachel said.

<Yes. That comet has to hit,> I said. I hated saying it. I hated thinking that the brave little settlement of Mercora was going to be destroyed. But this was destined to be a day of annihilation, and I'd known from the start we couldn't change history. All of this had already happened. Sixty-five million years before I was born.

Ax said, <They will have to drop the force field when their ship takes off. We will need to be in the air, ready to slip out.>

He was right. Tobias was right. I knew it. But it made me sick inside. And I wasn't the only one.

<You know, these guys saved us. Saved *me*,> Jake said. <I don't like this, running off like this. Maybe we could warn them. Maybe they could get away, get off the planet.>

<They lack the ships,> Ax said. <Their struggle with the Nesk has left them with only that one ship. Besides, what if they found a way to survive? We would have altered history in a very large way.>

<This stinks,> Jake said bitterly. <I don't run out on people who've saved my life.>

<You have no choice, Jake,> Tobias said.

<The ship is almost ready to launch,> Ax said. He'd been keeping watch with his stalk eyes.

<Now or never,> Tobias said.

<Now,> Marco said.

<Yes,> Ax agreed.

<No choice,> Rachel said, sounding more conflicted than I would have expected.

<Yeah,> Jake said. <It's really not up to us to rewrite history.>

I wanted to laugh. We acted like we were making a decision. But Tobias had already made the hard decision. The comet would not be stopped. The only question now was would we run away and try to live? We knew the answer to that.

<Thanks, Tobias,> I said.

I don't know if he thought I was being sincere or sarcastic. I wasn't sure myself.

I opened my wings and flew.

Chapter 36

 Jake

We flew. Up through the force field just as the doomed saucer lifted off.

The Mercora were all out to watch the ship take off. The ship that carried all their hopes with it. They didn't see us in the darkness.

I was mad at Tobias. I was mad at Ax for helping him. But I knew they'd done the right thing. My being angry was the proof of that. See, even though I knew Tobias was right, I could get mad at him. I could try and blame him for the tragedy that was about to occur.

Which meant I didn't have to blame myself.

We flew, up and up. It was dark and we swept past so quickly that the Pteranodons didn't even notice us. They were day hunters. Actually, so were we, in our bird-of-prey morphs. Our eyesight was not much better than human in the darkness.

We flew up and out of that valley where the funny crab creatures grew their broccoli. Up into sky untouched by any artificial light, and towards the ocean.

The comet was amazing, and I guess it would have been beautiful. If we hadn't known what it was. If we hadn't known what it meant.

We flew for close to our two-hour time limit. We demorphed, then remorphed as quickly as we could. This time Cassie and Rachel used their owl morphs, so they could guide us all in the darkness.

<How big a boom will this thing make when it hits?> Rachel asked.

<That depends on the speed of the comet and its size,> Ax said. <The Mercora have observed the comet. They say it is approximately eight of your kilometres across. It is approaching at a speed of twenty-five kilometres per second.>

<Per *second*?> Marco asked.

<Yes. When it hits it will release as much energy as, say, a million of the nuclear weapons on that submarine.>

<Excuse me? A million nukes?>

<Well, assuming the "nukes" are reasonably well-made examples of primitive nuclear technology. I am being very approximate,> Ax said. <There will be shock waves. One shock wave will go forward into and through the earth. It will compress the rock beneath it, which will release all the carbon dioxide trapped there. There will be a huge fireball from the exploding gases and from the vaporized comet itself. Everything within a hundred and fifty kilometres or so, every animal, every plant, everything, will be incinerated. There will be a huge crater, maybe twenty, thirty kilometres deep.

The second shock wave will bounce back from the impact. It will blow massive quantities of burning rock all the way out into space. These burning rocks will fall across a wide area. As they re-enter the atmosphere they will probably cause a massive heat wave, so hot that trees and grass will catch fire and burn. Any living thing out in the open will be cooked alive as—>

<Enough!> Cassie cried.

<Yeah. That's probably enough information,>

I agreed. <The question is, how do we live through this?>

<And are we sure we want to,> Tobias said darkly. <The next few years on planet Earth will not be fun. First fire, then darkness. Darkness and cold and death everywhere.>

<Look, I'm interested in surviving,> Rachel said. <Period.>

<The shock wave is the first threat, then the intense heat,> Ax said. <When the comet strikes, perhaps we should be in the water.>

<We're better off flying until the last minute,> I said. <We'll make more distance. We follow the coast north, then, at the last minute, we head out to sea.>

We flew. All through that night, only stopping to demorph every two hours. The sun rose over a scene of breathtaking beauty. We were over a river delta. A hundred glistening streams all heading for the ocean. And in that lushness, the dinosaurs. Slow Triceratops, and herds of huge Saltasaurus, the long-necked, long-tailed dinosaurs we'd encountered before. There were hadrosaurs and gigantic crocodiles and Pteranodons diving for fish.

Great, lumbering giants. It was a world where elephants would have seemed only average in size. Hundreds of species of dinosaurs, each a miracle of nature.

And yes, here and there as we flew we saw the tyrannosaurs and the other great predators. For some reason, although Tyrannosaurus had repeatedly tried to kill us, it was the Big Rex I pitied most.

They were so sure of their power. So confident. This was their planet and they were the kings. I wondered if they ever looked up and noticed that something was different in the sky. I wondered if they, too, saw the comet and felt a quiver of fear.

The comet was visible even in the brilliant daylight now. And it was beneath that comet, and above the teeming life of the Cretaceous, that we flew.

We rested at last in the high branches of a tree. All except Ax, who stayed below. Tobias was right at home there in the trees. And we humans could hang on and feel somewhat safe.

Cassie laughed a sad sort of laugh. "Well, here we are, just a few tens of millions of years early. Primates will evolve, and they'll learn to live in the trees, running from the sabre-toothed cats and other predators. And here we are now, just a little early."

"By now they know," Rachel said, looking back in the direction we'd come from.

"Who?" Marco asked her.

"The Mercorans. They know the nuke didn't go off. They know it's all over for them."

Marco nodded. "Yeah. I wonder if they know why? I mean, that we did it. I wonder if they've figured out that we didn't come from some far-off place, but from some far-off time on this planet. I wonder if they'll figure out why we . . . you know, *why*."

A Saltasaurus came by and stuck his snake head up into the tree, indifferent to us, and munched some leaves.

Night came again, and now we flew on urgently, desperate for every last kilometre. And finally, Ax said it was time.

We veered out to sea. We landed in the water, hoping that we could avoid being eaten in the few minutes that remained. We morphed to dolphin, and waited for the world to end.

Chapter 37

 Cassie

I stayed on the surface to watch the end.

The comet was a blazing torch as big as a mountain. It hit, and the entire planet shuddered from the impact. You could almost imagine Mother Earth crying out in pain. But you know, Earth is just a big ball of dirt and water and air and life, spinning through space. It's only important because it's ours. The universe didn't care that the orbit of Earth and the trajectory of a comet would intersect at this time and this place.

And yet in my mind, in my heart, I cried out for Earth.

The explosive power of a million nuclear weapons went off all at once. It was as if a giant had swung a hammer the size of the moon into our planet. I felt the impact in my insides.

The explosion seemed to rip the universe apart.

But I never felt the concussion. Because suddenly, I was no longer in the ocean watching the doom of the dinosaurs.

I was floating above it all. Floating in air, but not really. In space, only I could breathe.

<The *Sario Rip*!> I heard Ax cry. <The impact of the comet is collapsing it!>

But this time the travel through time was different. We weren't suddenly back where we started. We were hurtling through a void, hurtling past a video tape set on fast forward.

I saw the crater. It was a hole big enough to lose a dozen cities in. Flaming hot debris exploded outwards. A red-hot fireball rolled across the landscape, burning everything, a blowtorch on dry grass.

Trees exploded into flame. Dinosaurs crinkled and blackened and fell dead where they stood, no time even to cry out. The burning wind expanded outwards. The sky itself seemed to burn! But then the fireball weakened and from the wreckage rose smoke and dust. Earth was hidden by a blanket of smoke and dust. The sun was blotted out.

Earth began to freeze, and still more creatures died.

It was all passing before my eyes now, faster and faster. The sky cleared as acid rain fell, disintegrating many plants and starving the remaining dinosaurs. The plant-eaters were too few now.

I saw, in a flash, the last Tyrannosaurus, wandering hungry, thin, weakened and alone, across a blasted landscape. It was looking for the prey that was no longer there. And then it fell.

Time sped up, and the continents floated across the surface of the world. I watched Antarctica slide to the bottom of the planet and grow icy. I watched the Atlantic Ocean appear where only an inland sea had been. India broke away and then slammed violently into the bottom of Asia, rippling up the Himalaya Mountains.

Ice sheets advanced and retreated. Forests spread and withdrew and spread again. Mountains rose up sharp and craggy, then crumbled slowly to softer, smoother shapes.

And everywhere, the small, brown, fur-covered creatures increased in number. They filled the land the way the dinosaurs had. They migrated into the seas. They became plant-eaters and meat-eaters. Big and small, cute and deadly, slow and fast. And suddenly, there they were in the trees, swinging from branch to branch. And an instant later, some were banging rocks together and forming tools of bone and wood.

They walked erect, on two legs. They built huts and villages and cities. But all of this passed in a flash. Because in the long, long history of Earth, the entire history of Homo sapiens is not even the blink of an eye.

The dinosaurs ruled for a hundred and forty million years. Humans have existed for less than one million years.

I was in water again.

My friends were there, too.

I fired my dolphin echo-location clicks and "saw" ships in the water. And I felt the last, dying echoes of the underwater nuclear explosion that had first opened the *Sario Rip*.

<We're right back when we began,> Ax said.

We demorphed near the beach and when we climbed out, there was the boardwalk. It was still raining.

We went to our homes, dazed, awed, and watched the news reports of the terrible disaster at sea. A disaster that, fortunately, had not resulted in any deaths.

The Navy diver who was the hero of the rescue swore she'd been led to the submarine by dolphins. Some people suggested maybe she was suffering from hallucinations brought on by the depth and by breathing the wrong mix in her scuba tanks.

I returned to my life, feeling strange and out of place. That night Jake came over. We went outside.

"I tried morphing the Tyrannosaurus," he said. "Nothing. Didn't work."

"You could ask Ax. He may know why."

Jake laughed. "Yeah, but even if he explains it, I still won't understand it."

"Maybe it was all just a dream," I said.

"No. Not a dream," Jake said. "But it all happened a long time ago."

"Were we always there? I mean, were we meant to be there? To do what we did? Was everything supposed to happen a different way? Should this planet be ruled by the Mercora today? Or the Nesk? Should there still be dinosaurs stamping around? Did we make it all right or mess it all up?"

Jake didn't have an answer, so I slipped my arm through his. We looked up at the sky for a while. "No comet," Jake said.

"Not today, anyway," I said.

A note:

<Hi, it's me, Tobias. After we got back from our adventure in the late Cretaceous, I looked up some of the dinosaurs we encountered: Tyrannosaurus, Deinonychus, Saltasaurus, Spinosaurus, Elasmosaurus, Kronosaurus, and Triceratops. All of them were around during the Cretaceous Age. But paleontologists seem to think some of them, like Spinosaurus, were extinct by the *middle* Cretaceous, whereas we were in the *late* Cretaceous. All I can say is that I was almost eaten by a supposedly extinct Spinosaurus. So who are you going to believe? Me, or a bunch of scientists with some old fossils?>

19 The Departure

"Aaaahhhh!"

I woke up screaming.

I was in a boiling, mad, lunatic current. Water rushed around me, over me. Water filled the air. It twisted me over and over like a corkscrew.

I flailed my arms, but they barely moved. I couldn't feel my hands or fingers. My legs felt dead. I was freezing. Freezing to death.

THUMP!

I hit a rock and barely felt the impact on my side.

Then . . . falling, falling! I saw trees that seemed to fly up and away from me. I saw a glimpse of explosive white water beneath me. I was falling, the water vertical around me.

PAH-LOOSH!

I was all the way underwater, and being pounded viciously by the waterfall. It sounded like some monstrous engine, throbbing, beating, hammering at me.

FWOOSH! FWOOSH! FWOOSH! FWOOSH! FWOOSH!

I tried to swim, but my arms were made of jelly. My fingers were stiff as sticks. *Morph!* I told myself. But I couldn't concentrate. Couldn't hold the thought in my brain.

Suddenly, I shot clear of the beating waterfall, but I was still underwater. Far underwater. Too far.

I tried to hold my breath, but I was becoming more and more confused. What . . . where . . . which way should I . . . arms. . .

I sucked air into my burning lungs.

Only it wasn't air.

I gagged and writhed, helpless. Suffocating! My head bumped on something. A rock? The surface! I could see it. Now it was just centimetres over my head.

Just centimetres of water separated me from the air.

But it was too late. I closed my eyes. My muscles relaxed. I went to sleep.

I didn't feel the arms that hauled me up out of the water. I didn't feel the mouth that breathed air into me.

"Hah! Wah?" I woke up! Then instantly felt my insides heave.

"Buh-buh-leaaahhh!"

I threw up. I was on my back in the dirt. I vomited all over myself.

I rolled my head to one side and sucked in air, coughed, breathed, coughed some more. I hacked away for several minutes, gasping for a good clean breath with lungs still wet from the river.

A sharp pain in my side. A splitting headache. Pins and needles in my frozen hands and feet so intense it made me want to scream.

But I was alive!

Only then did I noticed the girl. She was squatting just a metre or so away. Her red hair was wet and bedraggled, plastered against her forehead and hanging in long, soggy curls.

She had brilliant green eyes that seemed unnaturally large. She was wearing jeans, a T-shirt, and a denim jacket. She was shivering.

"You saved my life, didn't you?" I said to her in a hoarse, raspy voice.

"You saved mine," she said. "That bear could have killed me. So now we're even. I don't owe you anything and you don't owe me."

It was a strange thing to say. Too mature . . . I don't know, too *old* to be coming from someone so young.

I sat up, fighting the urge to cry from the pins and needles feeling. "My name is Cassie."

"I'm Karen."

"Where are we?"

She shook her head. "I don't know. We were in the river for a long time. I was knocked out, too. But I came to sooner than you. And I was able to grab on to a floating log for part of the time."

I looked around. The trees were very tall, mostly pines. I saw no obvious trails. No rubbish or other signs of humans. We were deep in the forest.

I tried to form a mental picture of the course of the river. I knew it came down from the mountains, fed by melting snow and rain. It swept very near our farm, then doubled back, heading towards the mountains until the slope changed again and turned it at last towards the sea.

But that didn't tell me where we were. We could be a kilometre from civilization, or we could be ten kilometres. But more troubling was that I didn't know what direction to go. If we went the right way, we might hit a road pretty soon. If we went the wrong way . . . well, the forest was very large. You could be lost in the forest for a long, long time.

"Did you ever read *Hatchet* by Gary Paulsen?" I asked Karen.

"No."

"I did. I wish I'd paid more attention. I'm not exactly an expert on wilderness survival tactics. Besides, we don't seem to have a hatchet. Guess we'll just have to take our best guess and walk out of here."

Karen looked solemnly at me. "My ankle is hurt. I can't walk."

I took a deep breath. I was mostly revived now. I could feel my hands and feet again. And my brain was starting to work a little better, too.

"Karen, what were you doing there in the woods to begin with?"

She didn't answer. She just looked at me.

I felt a new kind of chill. "The other night, someone was behind the barn, looking up at my window. That was you, wasn't it?"

She said nothing.

I felt an awful dread begin to well up inside me. I felt like I couldn't breathe.

"Why were you following me? Why were you spying on me?" I demanded, trying not to panic, but already feeling the terror growing inside me, churning my stomach, squeezing my heart.

Karen sighed. Then she cocked her head and looked at me quizzically. Like I was some interesting specimen of insect and she was an entomologist.

"You interest me," she said.

"There's nothing interesting about me. Really."

"Sure there is. See, if I'm right about you, then you can fly away from this place any time you want. If I'm right about you, you can also . . . let's just say, make a few changes . . . and kill me."

I forced an awful fake laugh. "What on earth are you talking about?"

"Oh, nothing on *Earth*," Karen said. "At least that's what everyone believes. Humans can't morph. Only Andalites can morph. Only an Andalite could become a wolf and rip the throat from my brother's host body and leave him dying."

I guess Marco would have been cooler, more glib. Maybe Rachel would have just attacked. I don't know. But I'm not Marco or Rachel.

I stared, breathing stopped.

"I have no idea what you're talking about," I said.

Karen smiled a small, triumphant smile. "I followed you after that battle. You separated from the others and went your own way to that farm. I saw you loping along as a wolf one minute, then I lost sight for a few minutes. But when I caught up again, there was no wolf. Just you. Seemingly a human girl."

"What do you think I am? A werewolf or something?" I asked, trying out my desperate, fakey laugh again.

"I don't know what you are," Karen said. "Not for sure. That's why I followed you. See, everyone knows there's a band of Andalite warriors here on Earth. It makes sense that they would try to pass as humans. But everyone also knows no Andalite can stay in a morph more than two hours. And I've seen you in this human morph for more than two hours at a time."

I shrugged and put on a baffled expression. "OK, whatever. Maybe the cold water messed up your brain a little or something. Maybe we should just focus on getting you some help."

"I know you're not an Andalite who's been trapped in a morph because you morphed that wolf the other night. So that leaves two possibilities. Either you are an Andalite who has somehow figured out how to defy the two-hour limit. Or. . ."

"Or what?" I couldn't help asking.

"Or what some of us have suspected for some time is true: there are humans who can morph."

I shrugged. "Are you like one of those *X-Files* people?" I asked.

Karen smiled. "If you're an Andalite, you'll just demorph and kill me. This little human body would be defenceless against your tail."

"Now I have a tail?"

"If you're a human who can morph, then you'll morph something nasty and kill me that way."

"So, wait a minute. Let me get all this straight. In this little fairy tale of yours, I'm capable of destroying you either way, right?"

She cocked her head in a very human gesture. "You'll *think* you can," she said. "And whatever you do, I'll have proof."

I stood up. I'm not exactly tall enough to tower over anyone or look very threatening. But still, Karen should have looked just a little bit nervous. Instead she looked smug. Cocky. Like she was just waiting to see what I'd do.

I stuck out my hand. "Come on, crazy girl," I said, "let's get started. It may be a long walk back."

There was a flicker of doubt in those cool, green eyes. She ignored my hand and tried to stand. Halfway up, her left leg buckled and she fell back heavily.

"My ankle is badly injured," she said. "I'm afraid I can't walk."

I looked down at her and ran through my options.

In this forest there were bears and wolves. The bears wouldn't attack her as long as she stayed out of their way. But the wolves might, if they were hungry enough. The woods around us looked empty, silent. But I have been a wolf. I know the awesome power of their senses. I was willing to bet that at least one wolf pack already knew we were there. They'd heard us, they'd smelled us.

If they were hungry enough, they'd come by to check out the unfamiliar smell. If they came and saw a helpless kid, unable to walk, defenceless . . . well, wolves aren't man-eaters by nature, but they are programmed to take down the weak and sick.

And if the wolves didn't get her, there was the cold night and the hunger. If I walked away now, the human-Controller named Karen could very possibly not survive the night. Killed by nature's hand.

One thing was certain. If Karen made it back to her fellow Controllers, knowing what she knew, none of my friends were safe. She knew I was an Animorph. Or had been one. It would be easy for her to find out who my friends were. To take them, one by one, and make them submit to infestation. Make them into Controllers.

All it would take was one: me, Jake, Rachel, Marco. It didn't matter. If the Yeerks controlled one of us, all our secrets would be theirs.

They would learn of the hidden colony of free Hork-Bajir up in the mountains. They would learn about the Chee — the peace-loving androids who sometimes helped us with information.

If Karen came out of this alive, Jake, Rachel, Marco, Tobias and Ax would all be caught and made into human-Controllers or be killed. The Chee would be annihilated. The Hork-Bajir would be recaptured.

All hope for human freedom might die. Unless . . . unless Karen was destroyed right here, right now.

I turned away and walked to a dried-out, fallen tree. I grabbed a long, forked branch. I levered my weight against it and worked it until it splintered and cracked.

It was a strong, stout branch. One metre long, thick, with a fork at one end. I gripped it tightly and carried it back to Karen. One swift, sure blow to the head. That's all it would take. I could knock her out and leave her tied up with her own shoelaces and let nature do the rest.

I saw the apprehension in her eyes.

"Here," I said. "This will make a good

crutch. Wait here while I find some smaller sticks to make a splint."

We were not in a good position. Night was falling. We were somewhere in a forest. We had no tools and no matches. Everything around us was damp, maybe too damp to burn. And what I could see of the sky, looking up through the trees, was filled with dark clouds scudding on a stiff breeze.

"This will hurt," I said. I had found some sticks the right length. I had removed my belt. Fortunately, I never listen to Rachel on matters of fashion, so I had a good, strong, practical leather belt.

"Your trousers will fall down," Karen said, sounding like a kid again.

"Yeah, right. I seem to have gained a little weight since I bought these trousers. They're tight enough. Or maybe they shrank. That could be it." I placed the sticks carefully around her lower leg and down over her ankle bone. Then I wrapped the belt loosely. "OK, I'm not going to tighten it a lot, because your ankle is going to swell up. But I have to tighten it some. I want to keep your ankle immobilized. On the count of five, OK? When I get to five, I'll yank it. One. . ."

I yanked the belt.

"Aaahhh! Hey! What happened to five?"

"You would have tensed up on five," I said. "This way I caught you while you were relaxed."

"A trick."

"For your own good."

Karen snorted. "Now I know you're an Andalite. Typical Andalite arrogance. The only race in the entire galaxy that makes war 'to help people'."

I stood up again and stuck out my hand. This time, Karen took it. "Come on," I said. "We have to get moving."

I helped her to her feet. She winced in pain as she placed weight on the bad ankle. I leaned over awkwardly to grab the crutch. "Here. Try this."

She stuck it under one arm. "Which side? The side with the bad ankle, or the other side?"

"I don't know," I admitted. "I don't work with humans much."

"Ah? Ready to stop pretending and admit what you are, Andalite?"

I laughed. A real laugh this time. "I work with animals. I know how to set a broken leg on a deer or a racoon or a wolf. I've never done a human before."

Karen peered sceptically. "Ah, yes. The barn full of animals. Of course. What a perfect cover for an Andalite. All those animals right there so you can acquire their DNA for morphing."

"Whatever you say, kid," I muttered. "Let's try moving."

"Where are we going? Which way is civilization?"

"I don't have a clue. But it doesn't matter. We're not trying for a way out, not tonight, anyway. We need shelter."

"What? If you're going to try to kill me, go ahead and do it. No need to drag me off to some secluded spot."

"Karen, what could possibly be more secluded than this?" I waved my arm around at the tall trees.

"OK, if you don't have the stomach for killing me, let's walk out of here. My leg is fine." She took a couple of wincing steps.

"Look, I'm sorry you think I'm some space alien. I'm sorry you think I want to kill you. But the truth is, if we try and walk out of here tonight, we could end up dead. It's going to rain. Maybe even storm. You ever been in a forest in the middle of a storm? The ground will be mud. Lightning hitting the trees. Flash floods in the gullies. Cold. No way to build a fire. You wouldn't like it."

Suddenly Karen erupted in a rage. "Why do you keep up this stupid game? I know what you are capable of! I know what you did. You could morph to that wolf and easily kill me and then run out of these woods. Why are you playing this game?!"

I waited until she was done yelling. Then I said, "I see higher ground over that way. Maybe low hills. I can't tell, peering through these trees. Maybe we'll find a cave over there. At least we'll be away from this river. It could rise during the night, with the rain and all."

But Karen wasn't listening any more. She was staring up at a tree.

"What is that?" she asked in a worried voice.

I followed the direction of her gaze. There, lodged in a crook of an elm tree branch, was a crumpled, ripped body. The sweet face with the big eyes was lolled to the side.

"It's a young deer," I said.

"What's it doing up there?"

"The animal that killed it put it there for safekeeping."

"What kind of animal does that? A wolf? A bear?"

I shook my head. "No. But a leopard does."